THE BOBBSEY TWINS'
OWN LITTLE RAILROAD

THE BOBBSEY TWINS BOOKS

By Laura Lee Hope

"Hurrah, we're off!" shouted Freddie

The Bobbsey Twins' Own Little Railroad

The Bobbsey Twins' Own Little Railroad

By

LAURA LEE HOPE

GROSSET & DUNLAP
Publishers   *New York*

CONTENTS

THE BOBBSEY TWINS'
OWN LITTLE RAILROAD

CHAPTER I

THE FIX-IT MAN

"FREDDIE, I guess your train will have to go to the hospital," sighed Flossie Bobbsey.

She and her twin brother Freddie stood at the edge of the pond in the Lakeport park. Into the pond had just tumbled Freddie's small steam engine, the most important part of his electric train! Flossie was afraid that the water had ruined it.

"I never heard of a toy-train hospital," said Freddie. "Only big ones, where they fix great big trains that get broken."

When the children had asked their mother if they might play in the park, they had forgotten to tell her that they were taking the engine with them. Now they were sure they should have left it at home. After all, a toy engine was meant to run on tracks, not to be pushed over grass.

"I hope it didn't go out far," said Flossie. "Oh, Freddie, be careful!" she cried, as the little boy dashed into the water.

He located his precious engine and fished it out of the pond. Water poured from the smokestack, the engineer's cab, and the steam boiler.

Tears came to Freddie's eyes. It made no difference to him that he was standing knee-deep in water and probably had spoiled his shoes. To him, the engine was the most important thing in the world. And it was in a sorry state!

Flossie felt almost as bad as her brother did. She loved to play with the electric train set. The blond, blue-eyed, six-year-old twins often pretended to be engineer and fireman. At other times they would play conductor and baggage master.

"Maybe, Freddie, if we let the engine dry out in the sun, it will be all right," Flossie suggested hopefully.

Freddie shook his head. "Water ruins 'lectric trains," he said sadly.

As he waded out of the pond, pretty Miss Hall, who had charge of the children's playground, came over to him. Miss Hall was sorry the engine had taken an unexpected bath. She advised the twins to go home right away, and change Freddie's wet shoes and socks.

Flossie looked up at her. "Do you know where there's a train hospital?" she asked.

The young woman smiled and said, "No, I don't know of a toy-train hospital, but I do know a young man who likes to tinker with toy trains. Maybe he can fix it."

Miss Hall said his name was Clinton Power, and that he lived on the corner of Pine and Main Streets, not far from the park.

The twins thanked her and hurried off. At the park gate they met their older brother and sister, Bert and Nan, who had come to get them. Bert and Nan, who were twins also, were twelve years old. They were dark-haired and dark-eyed and did not look a bit like their small brother and sister.

"Freddie's engine went for a swim and got spoiled," Flossie spoke up.

"Your electric engine?" Nan cried. "Oh, Freddie, that's a shame."

"But we know where to get it fixed," said Freddie. "At Mr. Power's hospital."

Bert and Nan laughed and wanted to know where it was. Hearing that the "hospital" was at the corner of Pine and Main, they said it was on the way home.

"Let's stop there right away," Freddie suggested.

Nan thought he should go home and take off his wet shoes and socks, as Miss Hall had advised. His shoes were making a *sqush-sqush* sound, so Freddie agreed.

"But you mustn't go to the train hospital without me," he said. "It's *my* engine."

"Okay, we'll wait," Bert replied. "But hurry back."

Freddie ran as fast as his chubby little legs would carry him. When he burst through the back door, the Bobbseys' jolly Negro cook Dinah laughed.

"I declare to goodness, you never came through a door quiet-like in your whole life," she said. "What are you up to now, Freddie?"

The little boy said he was not up to anything, but he had to change his shoes before going to the hospital. This remark caused Dinah to go dashing after him up the stairs.

"What's this about a hospital?" she asked. "You'd better tell your mother!"

Mrs. Bobbsey met her small son at the top of the stairs. Freddie had to stop and tell her about the engine. Mrs. Bobbsey and Dinah laughed about Dinah's fright, then helped him hurry into dry shoes and socks.

When Freddie returned to his brother and sisters, they set off for Mr. Clinton Power's. They found his small house and rang the bell. The door was opened by a sweet-looking woman in a gingham dress. Hearing the twins' request, she said she was Mr. Power's mother and thought her son could fix the electric engine.

"Please come in," she invited them. "I'll call Clinton."

While she was gone, Nan Bobbsey glanced about the living room of the little house. Though it was neat and clean, the furniture looked quite worn and the curtains at the windows were faded. Nan decided the Powers must be poor.

In a few moments a young man with a crutch under one arm hobbled down the stairway. Clinton Power was good looking and had a nice smile, but he did not seem very strong. He said he was glad to see his callers.

"Mother tells me you've had some trouble with an electric engine," he added.

Freddie handed Mr. Power the toy engine, which was still wet, and told him what had happened.

"First we'll have to dry this," Mr. Power said. "Let's go out to my workshop."

He picked up his crutch, and the children followed him through the kitchen and outdoors to a small building behind the house. In it stood a workbench, above which hung a row of tools.

The young man plugged the cord of an air blower into a wall socket, and inserted the blower into the body of the engine. It made a hissing sound as it forced air inside Freddie's toy and dried it.

Mr. Power now surprised the twins by taking a few sections of track from a closet, fitting them together, and attaching them to the electric current. When he set the engine on the track, there was a crackle and snap, followed by a few sparks. But in a few minutes the engine was running as well as it had the day Santa Claus had left it.

"Oh, thank you, thank you!" Freddie cried gleefully, and the other children expressed their delight, too.

"We haven't any money with us," said Bert. "Will it be all right if Dad pays you tonight?"

Clinton Power looked surprised. "I'm very glad I was able to fix your brother's engine," he said, smiling. "I wouldn't think of charging for it."

"Is this a free hospital?" Flossie spoke up.

Mr. Power looked puzzled, so Flossie explained what she meant. Didn't he run a train hospital?

The young man laughed and said his workshop had never been called a hospital, but maybe it was, at that. Anyway, he liked to tinker and fix things for people.

Nan was sorry that Mr. Power would take no pay for his work. She was sure that he and his mother needed all the money he could earn.

As soon as the twins reached home, she went to her mother and told her how kind the lame man had been. Couldn't the Bobbseys do something in return?

"If Mr. Power will not take money," Mrs. Bobbsey said, "I have an idea. Dinah has made some delicious cream puffs for supper. How about taking some over to Mr. Power and his mother?"

"Oh yes," said Nan. "I'll go right away, so they can have them for dessert."

She ran downstairs and put several of the luscious cream puffs in a box. When Flossie learned what was going on, she decided to join her sister. As they went out the kitchen door, Freddie, who was playing with their black-and-white fox terrier Waggo, spotted the box. Hearing that they were taking it to the Powers, he said:

"I want to go, too. I'll take Waggo. He needs a walk."

Waggo was a lively dog, but he obeyed Freddie pretty well. Now he trotted along nicely as they went down the street.

For the second time that afternoon the twins rang the doorbell of the little house. This time, Mr. Power opened the door himself.

"Why, this is—" he began, but got no further.

Waggo had spied a cat in the hall. The dog leaped through the doorway, hitting the young man's crutch. It flew from under his arm, and he fell to the floor!

CHAPTER II

"OH!" gasped Nan Bobbsey, as she leaned down to help poor Mr. Power to his feet.

Together Freddie and Flossie picked up his crutch and handed it to him. Then Freddie dashed into the kitchen after Waggo.

The Powers' cat had jumped to a high window sill, and was hissing and spitting at Waggo.

"You bad dog!" Freddie cried. He grabbed his pet's collar and dragged him from the kitchen.

In the meantime, Mr. Power had limped to a couch, and Nan was apologizing for Waggo's actions. Of the four Bobbsey children, Nan was the one who worried most when something went wrong. She was very much like her mother, who always wanted to help people in trouble.

Bert enjoyed helping people, too, but most of the time his mind was on sports, which he loved. In this he was like his father and often went to the ball park with him.

8

Another place Bert never tired of visiting was Mr. Bobbsey's lumberyard. It was situated on Lake Metoka, where good-sized freighters docked to unload. Bert, and Freddie, too, never missed a chance to see the big ships.

Mr. Bobbsey had pet names for his small twins. Freddie was his Fat Fireman, because he loved fire engines. Flossie was her daddy's Little Fat Fairy. Indeed, she looked very much like one when she wore a party dress.

Now, as the Little Fat Fairy sat looking at poor Mr. Power, she felt like crying. Flossie knew the fall had hurt the lame young man although he would not admit it.

"I'll be all right in a few minutes," he said. "I just was shaken up a bit. And now tell me, what brought you children back so soon? Another broken engine?"

Nan grinned and went for the box of cream puffs which she had set on a table near the door. As she handed over the box, Freddie piped up:

"You did us a flavor, and one flavor deserves another."

Mr. Power laughed, as he opened the box. "Um, these look mighty good! I'll do you a favor any time."

"Our Dinah baked them," said Flossie proudly. "I hope they'll make you feel better."

"I'm sure they will," said Mr. Power. "If you don't mind, I'll eat one right now."

Mrs. Power came into the room. Being a good cook herself, she said she knew that these cream puffs were extra special. Smiling, she, too, took one from the box and ate it.

"Do you go to business like my daddy?" Freddie asked Mr. Power.

"No," the young man answered. A sad look came over his face. "I haven't a regular job. What I like to do most is teach, but I never had teacher's training."

"You mean teach school?" Nan asked him.

Mr. Power nodded. He said he would like to find a position as a tutor.

Freddie was puzzled. "Tooter?" he asked. "You mean like tooting a horn in a band?"

The young man and his mother smiled. Mr. Power explained that a tutor was a private teacher, usually with one special pupil.

"Are there many tutors?" Flossie spoke up.

"Oh yes, a good many," Mr. Power answered. "Children who are on the stage, or in movies or circuses, frequently have private teachers."

"You mean," said Freddie, "that those children don't have to go to school? They can have fun most of the time? Gee, I'd like that!"

Mr. Power said that besides tutors with one pupil,

there were also teachers who held special classes for children who could not attend school during regular hours. In the movies and circuses, for instance, the young actors often performed during the daytime. They had to learn their lessons when they were not busy.

"In the circus," Mr. Power continued, "a schoolroom is often set up in one of the big fancy wagons."

"Oh, I want to be a circus child!" exclaimed Freddie.

Mrs. Power said that when she was a little girl her family lived far from any school, so she had had a tutor.

"I still have the desk I used when I was your age, Flossie," she said. "Would you children like to see it?"

"Oh, yes," Flossie answered.

"It's up in the attic," Mrs. Power said. "I'll bring it down."

Nan offered to help her, and together they brought the high little desk and chair down to the living room. How cute they were, with colored pictures of children at play painted around the edges of them!

Flossie climbed onto the chair and opened the top of the desk. Inside the lid was a slate blackboard with a piece of chalk.

"Oh, I think it's just be-yootiful!" Flossie exclaimed. "I wish—I wish I could have a desk just like it!"

Mrs. Power's eyes twinkled. "How would you like to borrow it and play school?"

"Tutor school?" Flossie asked. "And you mean we can take it to our house?"

Nan was not sure they ought to borrow the lovely old desk. She knew Mrs. Power thought a great deal of it, and would feel very sorry if anything should happen to it.

"You will take very good care of the desk, I know," Mrs. Power said. "If you would like to take it along right now, I'll lend you our express wagon to carry it on."

She brought the wagon from the cellar, and the desk and chair were tied on top of it. Nan said she would see that nothing happened to them.

"Thank you very much, Mrs. Power," Flossie spoke up, and Freddie added that maybe he could learn his lessons at the tutor desk and not have to go back to school.

Mrs. Power laughed, then told the twins she had lots of other old-fashioned toys.

"Some of them belonged to my uncle," she said. "When he was a little boy, he loved fire engines and trains, just like you, Freddie. I'll show them to you sometime, perhaps when you bring the desk back."

Of course Freddie wanted to see the fire engines

and trains right away, but Nan reminded him that it was suppertime and they must leave at once. They said good-by and went down the street.

When the twins reached home, they set the desk and chair on the front porch. As soon as supper was over, they went outside to play with them.

"Let's pretend we're circus children," Freddie suggested. "I'm a tightrope walker."

He jumped to the porch railing and stood on one foot, his arms up. The next instant he began to teeter and Bert caught him just in time to keep his small brother from landing head first in the bushes.

"You'd better sit down at the desk," said Nan. "I'll be the tutor. First we'll have a riddle spelling game."

"I can spell," Freddie piped up. "C-A-T spells kitten."

"Cat!" Flossie corrected him.

"Well, if you wait long enough, the kitten will grow up," Freddie returned gleefully.

"Quiet, children, quiet!" said tutor Nan. "The riddle spelling game will be a poem."

On the blackboard she wrote R-A-I-N, and said:

> *"R-A-I-N spells rain.*
> *Now put a T in front,*
> *'Cause when you do,*
> *It spells* choo-choo.

"What's the word, children?"

"Water," Flossie giggled.

"No," said Nan. "Now don't guess. Look closely at the blackboard and tell me."

"Train!" Freddie shouted.

"Right."

Freddie announced that it was now time for him to do another circus act. The little boy made so much noise leaping over the porch chairs and swinging onto the hammock, which he said was his lifesaving net, that the commotion brought Mrs. Bobbsey to the porch.

"It's time Flossie and Freddie started for bed," she said, laughing. The small twins went into the house, complaining that the days should be longer and the nights shorter.

As Bert and Nan sat talking on the porch, there was a thud against the front steps. The twins looked up to see Danny Rugg, a boy Bert's age, picking up a baseball. He was laughing.

"Scared you, didn't I?" he said.

Bert and Nan did not like Danny, who was always playing mean tricks. They said, "Hello," and turned away.

Without being invited, Danny sat down in a chair on the porch. Seeing the old desk, he said:

"Where did you get that crazy-looking thing?"

"It doesn't belong to us," Nan answered. "And it isn't crazy. It's an old school desk and it's valuable."

Danny wanted to know why, if it did not belong to them, they had it there. Bert explained that it had been lent to them for a couple of days.

Danny stood up and looked at the desk a moment, then suddenly picked it up and started down the porch steps.

"Hey, what's the big idea?" Bert called out. "Bring that desk back!"

"Make me!" Danny sneered.

Bert leaped after Danny and tugged at the desk. He snatched it away and started up the porch steps. Danny grabbed at Bert's legs and he sprawled face down. The lid of the desk flew open.

With a laugh, Danny started to run off. Then he stopped, pulled the baseball from his pocket, and threw it hard. The ball just missed Bert, but hit the slate blackboard with a *whack!*

"Oh! You've cracked it!" Nan cried.

CHAPTER III

A WONDERFUL SURPRISE

DANNY'S unexpected action shocked Bert and Nan.
Fearfully they examined the old desk belonging to
Mrs. Power.

"This is dreadful!" Nan said, looking at the
cracked slate. "What will we do?"

"I know what we'll do!" Bert said angrily. "Make
Danny Rugg pay for this, even if I have to fight
him!"

Bert turned around to carry out his threat, but
Danny was not in sight. Bert dashed to the street
and looked up and down. Still he could not see him.

Concluding that Danny must have gone home,
Bert said he was going over to his house. But when
he reached it, Mrs. Rugg said her son was not there.
As a matter of fact, Danny had planned to spend the
night with his grandmother on the other side of
town.

"Why do you want him?" Mrs. Rugg asked.

Bert did not want to tell on Danny, so he said he would look for him at his grandmother's house.

But Danny was not there either. "I'll have to wait until tomorrow," Bert decided and returned home.

He found Nan talking to their parents about the desk. Mr. Bobbsey had examined it and said the slate blackboard could be replaced easily. Of course, it would not look exactly like the old one, but they hoped Mrs. Power would not mind.

"After all, it was not your fault," said Mrs. Bobbsey to the twins. "I think Danny should be made to pay for it."

Bert said he had been unable to find the boy, and they all wondered where he might be. How surprised the Bobbseys would have been, if they had known!

At this very moment, Danny Rugg was hiding among the thick bushes close to the porch where they were seated. He had crawled in there to get his ball, and had never had a chance to come out without being seen. Bert and Nan had not thought of looking for him there.

"It's too bad your evening has been spoiled," Mrs. Bobbsey said to the twins. "But Dad has a wonderful surprise for you. Why don't you tell Nan and Bert now, Richard?"

"I will," their father decided. "I was going to save

it until tomorrow, so all the children might hear it together. But I'll tell you two now about our wonderful gift."

Bert and Nan listened eagerly. Mr. Bobbsey said he had a friend named Dodge who used to live on a farm outside Lakeport. He had several children, now grown up.

"Mr. Dodge has sold his property for a housing development," Mr. Bobbsey went on. "He and his wife have moved into an apartment here in town. So they have no use for a wonderful toy which is in their old barn."

"A toy?" Nan asked.

"I suppose you'd call it a toy," her father answered. "But it's more than that. Grownups enjoy playing with it, too."

Bert could wait no longer. He asked his father to *please* tell them what the toy was.

Mr. Bobbsey laughed merrily. "Don't be so impatient, son," he said.

He kept on teasing the twins, saying the toy took up most of the space in the barn, but could not be used indoors. It had to be taken outside and set up. In case of rain, one could not play with it at all.

"Dad, you're an old meanie," said Nan, putting her arm around his shoulder. "Please, what is it?"

"A train."

"What?"

"It's a miniature railroad," Mr. Bobbsey explained. "The Dodge children used to play with it, I understand it has an engine, a tender, and a passenger car."

"And tracks?" Bert asked excitedly.

"Yes, several hundred feet of them."

"Let's go look at the train," Bert urged.

Mr. Bobbsey shook his head. He said it was too late to go that evening, but he would take the twins out there the next afternoon.

It was decided to keep the surprise for the younger twins until they actually arrived at the Dodge place the following day.

After the Bobbseys had left the porch and gone inside, Danny Rugg came out of the bushes and hurried off to his grandmother's. He had forgotten all about the blackboard he had ruined. He was busy thinking about the miniature railroad.

"The Bobbseys are too lucky," he said to himself. "They get everything. But I'll fix 'em!"

All the way to his grandmother's, Danny kept trying to figure how he could play a trick on the twins. Maybe he could go to Mr. Dodge's farm ahead of them. He did not know where the farm was, but perhaps his grandmother did. He would ask her.

Next morning Bert tried to find Danny, but the

other boy managed to keep out of his way. Finally Bert gave up the search and turned his thoughts to the train.

Just before lunch, he and Nan began whispering to each other. Freddie and Flossie wanted to know why.

Nan smiled. "We have a secret that you can't know about until this afternoon," she said.

"Can we guess what it is?" Flossie asked.

"Oh, sure," Bert answered. "Give you three guesses."

Flossie guessed that they were going somewhere in the car.

"That's right."

Freddie said it was on a trip.

"Not a very long trip," Nan replied. "But after we get out of the car, we might go on another kind of trip."

"A boat?" said Freddie.

"No."

Flossie guessed an airplane and a bus. Freddie finally said a train.

Nan did not know what to do. She had promised to say yes if they guessed right, but she did not want to spoil the surprise. Good old Dinah saved the day for her; the kindly cook said lunch was ready. The children went off to wash their hands.

The small twins were so hungry that they did not

talk at all during the meal. But as soon as it was over, they began teasing again to know what the surprise was.

"You've waited this long," said Mrs. Bobbsey, "I'm sure you can wait another two hours."

"But Nan promised—" Freddie began.

Once more Nan did not have to answer, because at that moment Mr. Bobbsey came in carrying a piece of slate. He asked where the little desk had been put. Nan went with him to the workshop in the cellar. It did not take him long to remove the broken slate and slip in the new piece.

"I believe this desk should be returned to Mrs. Power very soon," he said. "It's too valuable to be played with, especially when Danny's around." Nan said she would return it the next day.

Soon after lunch the children piled into Mr. Bobbsey's car and started for the Dodge farm. Their mother said she could not go because of a previous engagement.

"I'm going to take Marie," said Flossie, referring to her favorite doll.

When they reached the farm, Mr. Bobbsey parked at the side of the old barn. He told the twins to go around to the big sliding doors and wait. He himself opened a small side door with a key Mr. Dodge had given him.

He walked past the horse stalls to the main part

of the building, lifted the wooden bar from the big doors, and slid them back. In front of the twins stood the little railroad.

The children gasped, and Bert cried, "This is super! Gee, Dad, is this really and truly ours?"

The others rushed forward to look at the train. What a wonderful engine! It was exactly like a large engine, except that the seat for the engineer was up on top of the tender, back of the cab. It was plenty big enough even for Mr. Bobbsey to sit in.

"Oh, there's room for lots of people," Flossie cried, stepping into the passenger car. It had no roof but was quite long and had six seats in it.

Freddie already had climbed on top of the engine. He cupped his hand to his mouth and went *whoo-whoo-whoo* like a steam whistle.

"Let's go!" he shouted. "I'm the engineer of our Rootin' Tootin' Railroad!"

CHAPTER IV

THE LITTLE IRON HORSE

MR. BOBBSEY examined the engine of the "Rootin' Tootin' Railroad" and decided it was in good working order. He was sure that if water were put in the boiler and a fire built, he could get up steam to make the engine go.

"I'll help you," said Bert. "I'll get some wood to build a fire." He dashed from the barn and began gathering small pieces of dry wood.

Nan had noticed a little brook near by. Grabbing a pail from the corner of the barn, she ran for water.

Mr. Bobbsey laughed. "First we'd better see if these tracks are in good condition," he said.

The twins came back and helped him lug the heavy pieces outside. What a lot of them there were!

Fortunately none of the tracks were warped or broken. Mr. Bobbsey took some tools from his car, and bolted the pieces together.

"Now we're ready!" shouted Freddie, who had

been dancing around impatiently. "I want to sit up front with you, Daddy."

"Suppose you be my assistant fireman," his father suggested.

This suited Freddie perfectly. He helped Bert and his father push the engine from the barn. Getting it across the grass and onto the track was another matter. The little locomotive was very heavy, and the wheels would not turn, though the children and their father shoved and pushed with all their might.

"I guess we'll have to give up," said Mr. Bobbsey. "I'm beginning to think this miniature railroad will be too hard for you children to handle. Perhaps it should be in an amusement park where there would always be several men to manage it."

The twins looked glum. Flossie was the first to speak. "Daddy, we know lots of men. They'll help us. Please, can't we keep the train?"

Bert was down on his hands and knees looking at the stubborn little engine. There must be some reason why the wheels would not budge. Suddenly he noticed a rod which seemed to be locking the wheels. If it could be released, perhaps the wheels would turn.

"Dad, come and see this," he said.

Mr. Bobbsey got down and looked. Then he laughed, saying it was a good thing Bert had such sharp eyes. Reaching inside the cab, he pulled a lever and the rod moved, releasing the wheels.

"Our engine has a double-safety arrangement," he said. "It doesn't have to depend on steam alone to put on the brakes. It has a hand brake, too, like a car."

The engine was raised into position on the track. Water was poured into the boiler, and a fire built in the firebox, Freddie throwing in the sticks.

The small twins were impatient to start their ride, but Mr. Bobbsey reminded them that they would have to wait until the water boiled and made steam. It was the pressure of steam that moved the machinery and made the wheels go around.

While they were waiting, the children pushed the tender and passenger car from the barn and attached it to the engine.

"All aboard!" called Mr. Bobbsey a few minutes later, and sat down on the engineer's seat, which in this little train made him seem like a giant engineer.

The twins climbed into the passenger car. With a whistle from the steam valve, a *chug-chug*, and a little spinning of the wheels, the Rootin' Tootin' Train started off.

"Hurrah!" shouted Freddie. "We're off!"

Flossie clung tightly to her doll. "Oh, Marie, isn't this wonderful?" she cried.

"It's super!" Bert exclaimed. "Dad, will you show me how to run the engine?"

"After a while," his father promised. "I want to be sure all the gadgets work properly."

The train seemed just like a new friend to the Bobbsey twins, and they loved it already.

"The engine ought to have a name," said Freddie, as the little locomotive took a curve very steadily. It certainly held the track well.

"How about calling it the Iron Horse?" Bert suggested.

"It *is* an iron horse. It lives in a barn," Flossie giggled.

The others thought this a fine name, so the engine was dubbed the *Little Iron Horse*.

It was going faster now—fast enough for the breeze to blow back Nan's and Flossie's hair.

Freddie was terribly excited. He kept jumping up, and Nan had to pull at his shirt every few seconds to get him back on the seat.

Mr. Bobbsey was having a very good time, too. He enjoyed running the *Little Iron Horse*. Presently he called back:

"Maybe we should form the Rootin' Tootin' Railroad Company. What positions would each of you like to have in the company?"

"You said I could be the 'ssistant fireman," Freddie reminded him.

"I'd like to be the engineer," Bert answered.

"I'll just be a lady rider and watch the scenery," Flossie decided. "Marie needs my 'tension. She isn't feeling well today."

Nan was content to be a passenger also, for the present. After they had played with the *Little Iron Horse* awhile, maybe she would learn to run it, too.

When they had ridden around the circular track three times, Mr. Bobbsey brought the train to a stop in front of the barn.

"Now you try it, Bert," he said. He was sure his son could learn to run it easily, since there were only a few levers to push and pull.

Proudly Bert took the engineer's seat while his father explained which handle was the throttle and which was the brake.

"And watch this steam gauge," he cautioned Bert. "We wouldn't want our boiler to explode."

Off they went again, with Mr. Bobbsey sitting in the passenger car directly behind Bert. The *Little Iron Horse* seemed to know how to go round and round the track with very little direction from its young master.

"Gee, Dad," Bert said, "it would be a shame for us not to keep this swell train."

Nan had an idea. "Maybe, instead of giving it away, we could invite lots of children to enjoy rides with us," she said.

Mr. Bobbsey smiled and agreed to keep the Rootin' Tootin' Railroad, for the time being at least. As he said this, a boy came around the corner of the barn. "Your first visitor is here already," Mr. Bobbsey announced. "And it's Danny Rugg."

The twins looked up, amazed. How had he found out about the train?

Bert pushed the throttle, put on the brakes, and stopped the engine. His first inclination was to fight Danny, but he waited to learn why Danny had come to the farm.

Danny's first words were still more of a surprise. "Hello. Listen, kids, I'm sorry I broke the blackboard on the desk. I'll pay for it, if it doesn't cost too much."

The twins did not answer him, because Danny was used to getting out of situations in strange ways. They could not help wondering what was in his mind now. Bert suddenly thought it must have something to do with the Rootin' Tootin' Railroad.

"I'll bet he's just trying to be friendly so he can have a ride," Bert thought.

Mr. Bobbsey was pleased to see that Danny was sorry. He said it would cost Danny fifty cents for repairing the desk. Danny pulled the money from his pocket, but before handing it over, he said:

"I ought to get a ride on the train for all this money."

That was just like Danny, Bert thought. He knew it had cost his father much more than fifty cents to replace the blackboard. And furthermore, Danny wanted a ride for his money!

The children looked at their father. He was neither smiling nor frowning, so they could not figure out what he was thinking. He told Danny to take a seat in the passenger car.

Bert started off again. They had gone only halfway around the track when Danny called:

"Speed 'er up!"

Without thinking, Bert obeyed the command. Not realizing that he should open the throttle slowly, he made the train speed up with a jerk.

Flossie nearly tumbled out. The doll flew from her arms and landed with a splash in a small pond beside the track.

"Oh, Marie's drowned!" Flossie wailed. "Stop the train!"

Bert stopped the *Little Iron Horse*. All the Bobbseys hopped out to rescue poor Marie.

A mischievous look came over Danny Rugg's face. This was his chance to run the train himself! Stepping over into the engineer's seat, he released the brake, pulled the throttle, and the train chugged swiftly down the track. Hearing it, the others turned around and gasped.

"Stop!" Mr. Bobbsey cried, racing after Danny.

Before the twins' father could reach him, the little train came to a curve. Instead of slowing down, Danny made the engine go faster.

The next instant the *Little Iron Horse* jumped the track and toppled over!

CHAPTER V

A SHOWER OF HAY

AS STEAM hissed from the *Little Iron Horse*, Danny Rugg was thrown some distance away. He picked himself up quickly, and started to run.

The Bobbseys stood spellbound, expecting the engine to blow up any moment. But it merely kept on hissing.

As soon as their father was sure there was no danger, he hurried forward. Nan and the small twins raced after him.

By this time, Danny, frightened almost out of his wits, was racing as fast as he could toward the road.

"You won't get away with this!" Bert cried angrily, running after him.

Danny had a good head start. And he had left his bicycle at the road. Reaching the bike, he jumped on and sped off. Bert was not able to catch him.

When he returned to the others, Bert found that his father was using a tree limb to lift the *Little Iron Horse* to an upright position.

"I'll help you, Dad," Bert offered, and took hold of the limb.

Not only was the engine heavy, but now it was very hot. Even when the little locomotive once more stood on its wheels, Bert and his father could not get it back onto the track for fear of burning their hands.

"We'll have to wait until our horse cools off," said Freddie.

In the excitement Marie had been forgotten completely! Now Nan and Flossie went back to rescue the doll from the water.

"Here she is," Nan said, handing Flossie's bedraggled baby to her.

Flossie began to coo and murmur over Marie, promising her a whole set of new clothes for not getting drowned.

As they reached their father and the boys, the Bobbseys saw a man walking across a field toward them. He introduced himself as Mr. Haver, and said he lived on the next farm. He was a friend of Mr. Dodge's. Mr. Bobbsey explained that Mr. Dodge had given the miniature railroad to his children, and they had come there to try it out.

"We got into a little trouble," said Bert.

"So I see," Mr. Haver nodded. "Maybe I can help you get the engine back on the track."

"We didn't run it off," Freddie spoke up. "A

naughty boy did, and he ran away. But my brother will fix him."

Mr. Haver smiled, and said anybody who tampered with a railroad, big or little, should be punished. While they were waiting for the engine to cool off, Mr. Haver told them several stories about the little railroad, and remarked:

"You didn't set up all the track, I see."

Bert told him they had set up all the track that was in the barn.

"That's odd," said Mr. Haver. "I remember when the little railroad covered a quarter of a mile. It ran all the way around one of the fields."

"Maybe the rest of the track is stored somewhere else in the barn," Mr. Bobbsey suggested.

"Let's go find out," Bert urged.

They all went to the barn and searched every part of it. There was not a sign of any more track.

"If I were you," Mr. Haver said, "I'd ask Mr. Dodge where the rest of it is."

"Oh, I'm sure we have plenty," Mr. Bobbsey answered.

Mr. Haver explained that he was afraid the rest of the track might have been stolen. If so, surely Mr. Dodge would want to know about it. The twins' father agreed, and said he would notify him at once.

By this time the *Little Iron Horse* had cooled

off; in fact, the fire was out, and the steam down. Mr. Bobbsey thought it was hardly worth while to build another fire, so the little engine, tender, and car were pushed back into the barn. The tracks were taken apart and put away. Then the big barn doors were closed and the bar slipped in place. The side door was locked from the outside.

The Bobbseys thanked Mr. Haver for his help and said good-by. They drove home and excitedly told Mrs. Bobbsey and Dinah about their wonderful new toy.

"It's an iron horse and Danny knocked it over and steam came out of it, but it didn't blow up!" Freddie announced.

"My goodness, child," Dinah said, puzzled. "Whatever kind of horse is that?"

When she heard what it was, the cook laughed merrily.

"Marie jumped out of the train and most got drowned," Flossie reported, and she held up her dirty, half-dried doll.

Meanwhile, Mr. Bobbsey had telephoned Mr. Dodge. He was amazed to hear about the missing track. He had not given it away nor sold it, he said, so the track must have been stolen.

"I believe I'll get a police detective and go out there," he said. "Will you be able to go along?"

Mr. Bobbsey said he would meet Mr. Dodge at

the farm in an hour. He asked Bert if he would like to go, too.

"I sure would, Dad," his son replied. "I'd like to watch the policeman work."

He and his father met Mr. Dodge and a nice young police detective named Lynch. He started his work at once.

Bert was surprised that Detective Lynch did not hunt for clues to the missing track, like tire marks of a truck that might have carted it away. Instead, Mr. Lynch said he was looking for clues to identify the thief.

"What kind of clues?" Bert asked.

"Oh, something the fellow might have dropped, like a hat, or a handkerchief with a laundry mark on it. Then we could go to the hat store or the laundry and find out who he is."

But the policeman did not find any clues in the barn.

"What I can't understand," said Mr. Dodge, "is why anyone would want the track. It's certainly no good without the train."

Detective Lynch said maybe the thief was going to sell it for old metal. Anyway, they would put an extra lock on the side door. He took a padlock from his pocket, and snapped it on the door. He handed one key for it to Mr. Dodge and the other to Bert.

"I understand that the Rootin' Tootin' Railroad

belongs to you and your brother and sisters," he smiled, "so perhaps you should take charge of this key."

Bert was very proud to have the key and said he would take good care of it. Another thought came to him instantly. It would be exciting to get his friend Charlie Mason and come out to the barn with him. They would make an even more thorough search than the detective had. They would turn over every wisp of hay!

As soon as Bert arrived home, he telephoned to Charlie. Charlie was keen to see the Bobbseys' little railroad, and hunt for clues to the person who had taken part of the track.

"Let's get up real early tomorrow and go," Charlie urged.

"Okay with me," said Bert. "We'll go out there on our bikes. How about coming to my house at seven-thirty and eating breakfast here?"

"Swell."

Charlie came at exactly seven-thirty. He was a good-looking boy just Bert's age and height, and dark-haired like Bert. The boys sat down to breakfast with Mr. Bobbsey. First came fruit, then cereal, and finally small brown sausages and a platter stacked high with flapjacks.

When the boys had eaten enough to satisfy a whole search party, Charlie loosened his belt. "I'm calling quits," he groaned. "No room for any more."

"Me, too," Bert laughed. "Well, come on. Let's get started."

Mr. Bobbsey wished them luck. He made sure Bert had the keys to the barn. Then the boys pedaled off.

"Haven't you any idea who took the tracks?" Charlie asked as they neared the Dodge farm.

"No," Bert answered. "Nobody can figure out why a person would want the tracks if he didn't have the train to go with it."

"It sure is a puzzle," said Charlie. "Wouldn't it be swell if we could solve the mystery?"

The boys turned into the lane. Reaching the barn, they jumped off their bicycles and leaned them against the side. Bert unlocked the small door and slid it back.

"Listen!" he whispered. "I thought I heard something."

Both boys stood still, but there was not a sound.

"Probably a cat," said Charlie.

"Or a rat," Bert grinned. "Keep your eyes open, Charlie."

They stepped inside and walked directly to the main part of the building. As Bert lifted off the bar that locked the big doors, and slid them back to let in the light, Charlie exclaimed:

"Gee, this train is nifty!"

Bert did not answer. He was gazing at something he had not noticed the day before. There was a small pile of hay next to the passenger car. He lifted it up and his eyes bulged.

"Charlie, come here!" he cried.

Charlie dashed over and squatted down beside his friend. In Bert's hand was an old-fashioned watch and chain.

"A clue!" Bert shouted.

The next instant a tremendous shower of hay came down from the loft above. Both boys were completely covered by it.

As they struggled out, Bert and Charlie bumped into each other. Then Bert felt a hand against his own, and the watch and chain were yanked from him.

CHAPTER VI

THE SECRET WINDOW

COUGHING and sputtering, the boys cleared the hay from their faces.

"The watch!" Bert cried. "You haven't got it, Charlie!"

"Of course not. You had it."

"You mean you didn't take it?" Bert asked him.

"No," Charlie answered, bewildered.

"Well, someone did!" Bert cried.

He recalled the sound he had heard when opening the barn door. Someone must have been inside! He had pushed the hay down on the boys so he could take the watch and chain!

Bert and Charlie dashed outside. No one was in sight. The two bicycles were still there, so the person had not made his escape by riding off.

"He can't be far away," Bert said. "Maybe he's still hiding in the barn!"

The boys searched through the horse and cow

stalls, and the hayloft. At last they were convinced that no one was hiding in the building now.

Bert was glum. He had found a clue that might lead to the track thief, and now both the watch and the person hiding in the barn were gone!

Charlie was more cheerful. He walked over and moved the hay which had covered the boys. A grin spread over his face.

"You're in luck, Bert," he called. "That fellow didn't get the watch after all. Here it is on the floor!"

Bert leaped to his friend's side. "Gosh, that's swell," he said, as Charlie handed it over. "But the chain's gone."

The two boys sat down on the floor to study the watch.

"The man who owns it must be old," Charlie remarked. "My grandfather has a watch like this."

"Maybe the person who dropped it doesn't own it," said Bert. "He could have stolen it."

There were no initials on the watch to help locate the owner. Bert started to put it in his pocket to take to Detective Lynch. Then he thought of something.

"Let's open it and look inside," he said.

He tried to pry open the back of the watch with his thumbnail, but this did not work. Taking out his penknife, he inserted the small blade under the rim and finally managed to pry open the back of the watch. Inside the curved lid was a woman's photograph.

The boys stared at it. Neither of them had ever seen the face before.

"Do you suppose she lives in Lakeport?" Charlie asked.

Bert shrugged. The picture was a good clue, but it might take a long time to locate the woman herself.

"I'll tell you what," he said. "Let's go see Mr. Dodge. Maybe the watch belongs to him." He snapped the lid back on and put the watch in his pocket.

The boys slid the bar in place on the big doors, then walked to the small side door. Suddenly Bert stopped short.

"Say, Charlie," he said, "if somebody was inside this barn, how did he get in? The door had a new lock. He sure didn't have a key to it."

"You're right," Charlie agreed.

The boys concluded that there must be a window through which the intruder had climbed. They went out and looked around, but could not find any window with glass panes. However, Bert did spy a lengthwise, wooden panel which at first glance looked like part of the trim on the building.

"It might be a wooden window," Bert surmised.

The boys reached up and shoved it sideways. It

was a window, indeed, and large enough for a slender person to crawl through.

Charlie grinned. "You've solved part of the mystery," he said. "A thin man could easily get inside the barn through this opening."

"And drop pieces of train track out," Bert added.

He thought they should nail the wooden window shut, but they could not find nails or a hammer anywhere in the barn. Bert finally picked up a small piece of log and suggested they use it as a wedge. Returning to the inside of the barn, they closed the wooden window and jammed the log in tightly.

"Now nobody can get in here," Bert said confidently.

He locked the small door and the boys hopped onto their bicycles. They hoped Mr. Dodge would be at his apartment in Lakeport. He was not there when they arrived, but Mrs. Dodge said she was sure the watch did not belong to her husband.

"I don't recognize this woman," she said, looking at the photograph. "She has a very sweet face. I hope that the fellow who stole the tracks is not a relative of hers."

Just as the boys were leaving, Mr. Dodge drove up. He, too, had never seen the watch nor the woman in the photograph. He praised the boys for finding the clue, and said he hoped Detective Lynch would be able to use it to solve the mystery.

"I was just talking to him a few minutes ago," Mr. Dodge added. "He won't be back at police headquarters until late this afternoon. Suppose you take the watch to him then."

As the boys rode off, Charlie announced that he was very hungry. He wished he might have some more of Dinah's wonderful flapjacks, but he had promised his mother to be home by lunchtime. As they came to his house, he called to Bert:

"Let me know if you hear anything."

"I sure will," Bert promised. "See you soon, anyway."

When Bert pedaled into the Bobbsey driveway, Freddie and Flossie rushed from the back yard to meet him.

"Did you find the bad man who took the tracks?" Freddie asked, jumping up and down.

"No, but I almost did," Bert answered. "He ran away."

The small twins followed him into the house, where everyone, including Mr. Bobbsey, who had come home to lunch, eagerly listened to Bert's story. Freddie was too excited to sit still. He stood in front of Bert and took in every word.

"I wish I'd been with you," he said.

Flossie scoffed at this. "The bad man would have put hay on you, too," she said. "I'm glad you weren't there."

Not one of the Bobbseys recognized the woman in the picture.

Nan had a suggestion. "We have to take the desk back to Mrs. Power today. Let's show her the picture, too," she said. "She knows lots of people we don't know. Her son does, too."

After luncheon Bert tied the little desk and chair to the express wagon, and the four children pulled it to the Power home. The lame young man and his mother were surprised that the twins had brought it back so soon. Nan explained the reason for the new slate and said they did not want anything more to happen to the valuable old desk.

"We're terribly sorry about the accident," she added. "We tried to take good care of the desk."

Mrs. Power said she was sure they had, and the accident did not matter. No doubt, the new slate was far better for writing than the old one.

Bert took the watch from his pocket and asked the Powers if they knew the owner. They shook their heads, but when Bert opened it and showed them the photograph, Mrs. Power said:

"Why, that looks like Agnes Smither."

Bert became excited. "Where does she live?" he asked. "I'll take it to her right away."

Mrs. Power smiled a bit sadly. "Agnes Smither died several years ago."

"Oh," said Bert.

Nan asked whether Agnes Smither had any relatives whom they might go to see. Perhaps one of them could help the children find out who had dropped the watch in the barn.

Mrs. Power said that Miss Smither's parents were dead also.

"Didn't she have a brother?" Mr. Power spoke up.

"That's right," his mother agreed. "His name was Ray. Yes, Ray Smither. So far as I know, he's still living. But I have no idea where he is."

"The policemen will find him!" Freddie declared.

Bert, too, was confident this fine clue would solve the mystery of the missing tracks. What a lot he would have to tell Detective Lynch!

CHAPTER VII

A ROOTIN' TOOTIN' PICNIC

THE BOBBSEYS thanked the Powers and started down the street. Bert said he was going at once to see Detective Lynch at police headquarters, and hurried off.

When he arrived home shortly before six o'clock, Bert said the detective was glad to have the watch with the picture in it. He would try to find out whether the photograph really was of Miss Smither. And if it were, perhaps it would help him find her brother Ray.

During supper, the Bobbsey twins were buzzing with excitement over the Rootin' Tootin' Railroad. Nan said that several of her friends wanted to see it. Flossie's friend Susie had asked to ride in it, and Freddie had already promised Teddy Blake he could have a free ticket.

"I know what let's do," said Nan. "Let's have a picnic at the old barn for all our friends, and give them rides."

46

After supper what a rush there was to plan the list of guests!

"I'll make invitations," Nan offered. "I hope I can draw a train that looks like a train."

"You draw very, very good pictures," Flossie said loyally.

"What are we going to say on the invitations?" Bert asked.

Freddie had an idea. "Let's say: 'Write right back if you can ride on our track.'"

Flossie giggled. "You don't say where to go or what day," she reminded her twin. "Let's say: 'Come and play on Saturday.'"

Freddie thought this invitation was no better than his. It did not say where they would play, nor on what. Finally he and Flossie decided to leave it to their big sister and brother.

On one side of a piece of paper Nan drew a picture of a little train. Flossie declared it looked just like their own.

Nan creased the paper in half, and then sat wondering what to write on the inside of the invitation. Bert helped her and finally they put down:

> *Come to our picnic on Saturday*
> *Out at the old Dodge Farm.*
> *Take a ride on our Iron Horse*
> *That lives in the big red barn.*

At the bottom Nan printed in big letters: THE BOBBSEY TWINS.

"Now that's right pretty and smart," said Dinah, who had come into the room. "How many folks are comin' to the party?"

"Well, I'll have Grace Lavine and Nellie Parks and . . ."

"And all my friends," said Flossie. "And Freddie's and Bert's."

Nan went on counting silently. She used up all her fingers, started over again, used them up again, and finally got to twenty-four.

"And four of us Bobbseys makes twenty-eight," she said.

"That's a lot o' folks," Dinah remarked. "I guess we'll have to have sandwiches."

"We ought to have ice cream," said Nan.

"And cake," Dinah grinned.

Nan worked hard next day on the invitations. By late afternoon she had the drawings finished. That evening she and Bert wrote in the little poem, and addressed the envelopes. They mailed them in a box on the corner of their street.

By ten o'clock the following morning the young friends of the Bobbsey twins began to telephone them.

"I have your cute invitation," Grace Lavine told Nan. "I can hardly wait for the party."

"I laughed when I read about the Iron Horse," said John Marsh to Bert. He giggled. "Does he eat iron grass?"

"Sure, and gets all steamed up," Bert answered. The children's friends asked questions about the little railroad, but not one of the twins would tell a thing about it.

"Wait and see," was all they would answer.

Charlie Mason also telephoned. He said Danny Rugg had found out about the Iron Horse picnic and was angry because he had not received an invitation.

"Maybe we should have invited him," said Nan kindly, when Bert told her about it.

"Nothing doing," Bert answered. "He might pull another mean trick."

Saturday was a beautiful day—just the right kind for a picnic. Mr. and Mrs. Bobbsey, the twins, and the doll Marie, now spic and span, left for the Dodge place at nine o'clock. They took the sandwiches and cold drinks. Sam, Dinah's smiling husband, who drove a truck for Mr. Bobbsey's lumberyard, would drive over later with the ice cream and cake.

Charlie Mason met the Bobbseys at the farm to help set up the Rootin' Tootin' Railroad. As Bert unlocked the side door of the old barn, he suddenly had a sinking feeling in his stomach. What if the thief had come back and taken more track!

But Bert need not have worried. Everything was in place just as they had left it. The big doors were opened, and Mr. Bobbsey carried out the first piece of track. Bert and Charlie followed, and even Freddie was able to drag one section along the ground and lay it in place.

The twins' father began bolting the pieces together and soon the circular track was ready for action. Charlie was impatient to have his first ride, so as soon as the train was in place, and steam was up, Bert took him round and round on the iron rails.

"This is tops!" cried Charlie. "Gee, you're lucky to have it."

"I guess we are," Bert grinned.

During the next hour Mr. Bobbsey kept a low fire going in the locomotive. All the children gathered wood until Mrs. Bobbsey remarked that it looked as if they had enough wood to run the train for three days without stopping!

At eleven o'clock the guests began to arrive with their parents. Although the grownups had not been invited to the picnic, many of them stayed to watch the *Little Iron Horse* at work. Some of them even climbed into the passenger car and rode around.

Mrs. Bobbsey laughed. "I guess when it comes to trains, we never grow up," she said. "I'm glad our Iron Horse is strong."

At noontime she and Nan took the hampers and boxes of food from the car. Bert told his mother about two sawbucks and several boards he had seen in the old barn. He brought them out and set them up as a long table. A flowered paper tablecloth was spread over it, and the sandwiches and cold drinks were put out.

The excited children did not want to sit down at the table. They would eat a sandwich and drink a little milk, then go back for another turn on the little railroad. It seemed as if they could not get enough rides!

But when Sam arrived a little later with the ice cream and cake, all the guests ran up to get their share. When Sam set two large cakes on the table, they laughed. One had a design in the icing of an "iron horse" eating a sandwich through his smokestack. On the other cake he was drinking a bottle of milk through the steam whistle.

When everyone had finished their dessert, Mrs. Bobbsey suggested that the boys and girls who were waiting for rides play hide-and-seek. The children Freddie and Flossie's age were first.

Susie Larker was *it*. As she started to count to a hundred, the others ran off. Freddie Bobbsey and Teddy Blake hurried toward the old Dodge house. Freddie had never been there, and he thought this would be a good chance to see it. He could run faster than Teddy and soon was several yards ahead of his little friend.

Suddenly Teddy screamed. Freddie had disappeared. The ground had swallowed him!

CHAPTER VIII

A BROKEN ENGINE

AT FIRST everyone thought Teddy Blake's scream was part of the hide-and-seek game. But when he came running back to the barn, crying, "Freddie's gone! Freddie's lost in a big hole!" the grownups rushed to find out what had happened.

"Where is he?" Mrs. Bobbsey cried frantically.

Teddy led them back to where Freddie had disappeared, and pointed.

"Freddie's down in there!" he sobbed. "Get him out quick!"

Mr. and Mrs. Bobbsey looked into the hole and called Freddie's name. There was a muffled reply. They could see dirt and sod moving, and a second later the little boy's head appeared.

"G-get me out!" he wailed. "I'm stuck!"

Mr. Bobbsey reached down but could not quite touch his son's upstretched hands.

"I'll find something to pull you out, Freddie,"

he said. "Keep very quiet, so you won't sink in deeper."

By this time Bert and several of the older children had gathered at the hole. Mrs. Bobbsey warned them to stand back, or they might cause a worse cave-in, which would bury Freddie completely.

"I'll get a rope, Dad," Bert offered. "I saw one up in the haymow."

He fairly flew back to the barn and scooted up to the loft. In a jiffy he had the rope and ran back to his father.

Mr. Bobbsey put a slip noose in one end of the rope and lowered it to Freddie. He told the little boy to put it under his arms. Freddie did, and Mr. Bobbsey and Bert pulled the frightened child from the hole.

Poor Freddie was a sorry-looking sight. Not only was he dirty, but from his hips to his toes he was covered with mud.

"Oh Freddie!" cried Flossie. "What made you fall in?"

"This must have been an old well," said Mr. Bobbsey. "Evidently someone filled in the well with dirt and covered it with sod. But over the years the dirt settled and left only a bridge of sod over the top of the hole."

By this time Sam had come up. He found Freddie crying because Mrs. Bobbsey had said he would have to go home for a change of clothes. The kindly colored man offered to take him there and back in a hurry.

"I'll get you in and out of a shower faster'n a bird can take a bath," Sam grinned. "Then Dinah'll get out your clean clothes and I'll have you back here in time to get *home free*."

As the two drove off, Mr. Bobbsey said he would inspect the area around the barn thoroughly to be sure it was safe before the hide-and-seek game proceeded. He found no more holes. Then once more, Susie Larker started counting to a hundred.

Some of the older children decided to play cowboys and Indians. The grounds back of the barn were to be Dodge Town, a Western village.

Suddenly "Indian" Ned Brown spied Flossie's doll Marie, propped up against the side of the barn. With a war whoop, he raided the "village" and swooped down on the defenseless "child."

"*Wa-hoo wa-hoo wa-hoo*," he yelled, dashing off with Marie.

Flossie shrieked. She was not in the game, but this was very real to her. Marie might be injured a second time!

At once the cowboys were after Indian Ned Brown. Cowboy John Marsh galloped on his make-believe horse after Marie and took her away from the Indian.

Flossie rushed up and grabbed her baby. "If you

want to play stealing children, you can bring your own dolls!" she cried out.

The boys laughed at the thought of playing with dolls—which they had just been doing! But they agreed to leave Marie alone.

While the games were going on, Bert was showing Charlie how to run the engine. In a few minutes Charlie was sure he knew how.

"Let's go for a trial run," he suggested.

He was thrilled to push the throttle and hear the wheels spin for a moment. Then the *Little Iron Horse* gathered speed. They had gone around the track twice and were just leaving the barn, when Freddie's friend Teddy Blake ran to hop aboard.

Fearful that Teddy would be hurt, Charlie tried to stop the train. In his excitement he not only pulled hard on the hand brake, but swung a lever beneath the steam gauge. The train stopped with a tremendous shiver. Steam spouted from beneath the wheels.

"Oh, I hope I haven't broken anything!" Charlie exclaimed.

Bert climbed to the engineer's seat and tried to start the train. It would not budge. After several failures, he called to his father. Mr. Bobbsey could not get the *Little Iron Horse* to go an inch.

"I'm terribly sorry," said Charlie, as the other children crowded around. "Gee, I didn't mean to ruin the party."

Mr. Bobbsey and Bert told him not to worry. If they only knew more about the machinery, they probably could locate the trouble easily.

"My daddy's a train expert," Susie Larker spoke up.

"He is?" Charlie asked.

Susie explained that her father built model trains. They were just like real trains, and she was sure he could fix the *Little Iron Horse*.

Mr. Bobbsey looked at his watch. It was nearly four o'clock, the time set for the guests of the Rootin' Tootin' picnic to be picked up by their parents. Mr. Larker would be there shortly.

When he arrived, they asked him to examine the little engine. Mr. Larker worked on it for nearly half an hour but could not locate the trouble.

"I thought I knew a great deal about engines," he said. "But this one has me puzzled. I've never seen one just like it."

"'Cause there's not another one like it," called out Freddie, who had just returned to the picnic. "There's not another Rootin' Tootin' Railroad in—in the whole world!"

Mr. Larker smiled. "I guess you're right, Freddie," he said. "I give up. But I'll tell you the name of a young man who can probably find out in a jiffy how to make this little engine run again."

"Who is he?" Bert asked.

"His name is Clinton Power."

"Oh, we know him," the Bobbseys chorused.

Bert told how Freddie had taken his toy electric train to the young man, who had fixed it in a few minutes.

"I think," said Mr. Larker, "that if Clinton Power were not lame, he might work on large locomotives. But it is too tiring for him to stand up long."

Nan mentioned that Mr. Power wanted to become a tutor. Susie's father said he liked Clinton very much and hoped the young man would find a good position. Then he drove off with Susie.

Mr. Bobbsey said he would drive over to Mr. Power's house at once. "Perhaps he can come back here and fix the engine before we put it away," he said. "Come along, Bert."

They drove to the young man's home. Mr. Power gladly consented to look at the *Little Iron Horse.* He got a bag of tools and they set off.

By the time they returned to the barn, most of the children had left. The Bobbseys and Charlie Mason gathered around Clinton Power to watch him work.

After examining everything he could see as the engine stood upright, he said he would have to take a look underneath. It would be best to dump the ashes and let the water out. This was done.

Then the *Little Iron Horse* was laid on its side.

Mr. Power got down and poked into the machinery. "Here's your trouble," he said at last.

Using a pair of pliers, he unbolted several nuts and took off a rod and a little wheel. Reaching his hand inside where the others could not see, he pushed with all his strength against something and said, "There!" Then he replaced the pieces he had removed, and asked that the engine be lifted back on the track.

Water was poured into the boiler and a new fire was built. The group sat down to talk until steam was up.

After a while Mr. Power walked over to the *Little Iron Horse*, saying, "Now we'll try this out."

Everybody wondered if the engine would work.

CHAPTER IX

THE TINY CIRCUS PARADE

TOOT-toot-toot-toot-toot!

The whistle was working, anyway, thought Bert. Mr. Power must have expected the little engine to run, because the signal of several short toots meant *Clear the track!*

Very slowly he pulled the throttle back, and the wheels spun.

"It's going to go!" Freddie cried excitedly. "It's not broken any more!"

Everyone felt relieved, especially Charlie. As the wheels continued to spin, Clinton Power said they should put some sand on the tracks.

"This engine doesn't have a sander," he remarked.

Then he explained that whenever the wheels on a big locomotive slip, the engineer reaches for the sander valve and drops some sand on the track to give the wheels a better grip.

Bert found a small pile of sand near the barn and

sprinkled some of it on the tracks. In a moment the *Little Iron Horse* started moving.

Nan was sure that Mr. Power would not take any money for his services. But she made a decision. She would do everything she could to find him a tutoring position. Surely there must be children who needed a private teacher.

After several rides around the track, Mr. Power declared the engine was in good working condition. The twins' father said that since it was growing late, they would dump the fire and drain out the water once more.

While the engine was cooling off, the tracks were unbolted and put away. Next the tender and passenger car were rolled into the barn, and finally the *Little Iron Horse* was shoved in.

Before locking the doors, Bert examined the wooden window which he and Charlie had discovered. The stout wedge was still in place. He showed it to his father, who felt that breaking into the barn would be very difficult. He was sure the Rootin' Tootin' Railroad was safe.

On the way home Mr. Power told several interesting stories about famous locomotives, and explained how some railroads in the United States were built.

"Did you know the Pony Express became a railroad?" he asked.

Freddie's eyes opened wide. "You mean a pony grew up to be an iron horse?" he asked, and everybody laughed.

Mr. Power said that long before a railroad was thought of in the Western part of the United States, mail was carried on fast ponies. The riders wanted to get to the end of their trips as soon as possible, so they rode their ponies over the shortest and best route. It was called the Pony Express. Later, when a railroad was going to be built, the engineers decided to use part of the trail of the Pony Express.

"I see," said Freddie. "Tell us some more stories."

"Do you know why locomotives are sometimes called by numbers?" the young man asked.

The children shook their heads.

"Your *Little Iron Horse* might be called a One-Two-One engine," said Mr. Power.

Flossie giggled and asked if this meant how many legs the horse had because one and two and one made four. Mr. Power said in a way this was right. Sometimes the big iron horses had as many as thirty-six "legs." This meant eighteen on each side.

"Of course, I really mean wheels," he said, winking at Flossie. "At the front of an engine are the small pilot wheels. In the center are the big drive wheels, and in the rear are the little trailing wheels.

The famous Old Six-Six-Six had six wheels in each place on each side."

"And our little engine has one in front, two in the middle, and one in the rear," said Freddie. "So it's a One-Two-One. Is that right?"

"Absolutely right," Mr. Power replied.

Mr. Bobbsey stopped in front of the young man's home. He thanked him again for his help, then drove to the Mason house. After leaving Charlie there, the Bobbseys went home. Freddie and Flossie ran at once to the kitchen to tell Dinah what had happened to the *Little Iron Horse.*

"But it's fixed again," said Flossie. "Mr. Power knows just everything."

Since supper would not be ready for some time, Bert went to police headquarters to talk to Detective Lynch. The policeman had no news to report, although he had talked with shopkeepers and former neighbors of Agnes Smither. No one could tell him where any of her family was living.

"But I won't give up," he said. "A detective never gives up a case until it is solved."

"You mean," said Bert, "that you keep on looking for somebody for years and years?"

The young man nodded. "It begins to look as if this mystery of the watch and the photograph might be a long one," he said. "And it won't surprise me if you solve it before I do, Bert."

The boy grinned. He hoped the detective was right! He would hunt for more clues next time he went to the Dodge place.

On Sunday afternoon the twins walked over to call on Mr. Power and his mother. They hoped she would show them her old-fashioned toys. It was not long after they arrived that she said:

"I'll bring down some of the pull toys my mother and uncle used to play with. In those days there were no automobiles or motor trucks, so their toys don't look like the ones you play with today."

She was gone a few minutes. When she returned, Mrs. Power set a red fire engine on the floor. It was drawn by four white horses. She gave it a push. Away it rolled, but the horses' legs did not move!

Freddie got down on hands and knees to see why this was. He began to laugh.

"The horses have wheels under their stomachs!" he shouted.

When the horses and fire engine stopped moving, he gave them another shove. Then Flossie took a turn. The small twins were more interested in watching what they called the *stomach wheels* going around than in anything else on the toy.

Mrs. Power had been holding a box in her other arm. As she opened it, she said:

"Here are circus wagons for a parade. They're all pulled by horses."

First she took out a lions' cage. When Flossie pulled it along the floor by a string, the two lions behind the bars turned from side to side and looked very ferocious.

Next Mrs. Power set down a bandwagon. Sitting on top of the wagon were several musicians, each playing a different kind of instrument. Freddie liked best the one with the big drum.

"Pull it," suggested Mrs. Power.

As Freddie dragged it over the floor, the musicians pretended to play. The only one that made a sound was the drummer beating a soft *tap tap*.

Next came a chariot, then a calliope and finally several wagons, some with animals, some with clowns.

"Oh, the clowns are doing tricks!" Flossie exclaimed, as one bowed and another did a somersault.

Nan was intrigued by the circus parade. She thought the collection must be worth a good deal of money, and asked if this were so.

"I suppose it is," Mrs. Power answered. "But I prize the toys mostly as family heirlooms."

A caller came to the house at that moment so the twins left, saying they would like to come again some time and see the rest of the old toys.

"We didn't see any trains," Freddie remarked. When they reached home, he asked his father how soon they could run their own little railroad again.

Mr. Bobbsey said he would not be able to set up the train for several days, but if the children wanted to go out to the farm to play, their mother might drive them there. Mrs. Bobbsey said she would take them out to the farm the next afternoon. Then to Freddie, she added:

"If you promise not to tumble into any more holes! Watch where you're running."

Freddie laughed and said he would run as straight as straight. This was his favorite expression when he was promising to keep out of trouble.

As the twins and their mother reached the Dodge place the next afternoon, they gasped in amazement. The building work had started!

In the field where the railroad had been running, a bulldozer was digging up the soil and moving stones. Already a large space had been cleared.

"Oh dear!" Flossie wailed. "Now we can't have any more train rides!"

All the children felt bad. They had not expected the ground to be torn up so soon. Anyway, the barn would remain and they could keep the train in there until they could find another place for it.

Flossie had hopped out of the car with Freddie. Now they ran to the edge of the field to watch the man with the bulldozer. He was expert at making it go forward a few seconds, then backward, then turn a complete circle in a jiffy.

"Oh, Freddie!" cried Flossie suddenly. "I see something shiny. I'd better get it 'fore that man runs over it."

The little girl leaped forward through the lumpy field. As she reached the shiny object, Flossie tripped and fell flat.

At that very instant the man, who had not noticed the children, put the bulldozer in reverse and backed up directly toward Flossie Bobbsey!

CHAPTER X

A TREASURE HUNT

AS THE bulldozer kept on backing, Freddie screamed. So did Nan, who raced toward her little sister.

Bert shouted, "Whoa! Stop!" as loudly as he could.

Mrs. Bobbsey started running faster than she had ever run in her life, crying:

"Flossie, get up! Run!"

Poor Flossie! She could hear nothing above the roar of the bulldozer. But the driver did. He turned his head and stopped the big machine. The little girl was safe!

The man stepped down from his bulldozer. He had had a bad fright, but now his fright turned to anger.

"What are you kids doing here?" he cried. "You have no business getting in my way."

"I didn't mean to get in your way," Flossie whimpered. "You were going the other way when I came out to get the shiny thing."

"What shiny thing?" he asked.

Flossie looked around, then pointed. The man went over and picked up the shiny object.

"You mean this is what you nearly got run over for?" he exclaimed. "It's nothing but a piece of broken glass."

By this time Mrs. Bobbsey and the older twins had reached Flossie. Her mother hugged her, then turned to the man.

"I'm dreadfully sorry we caused you this trouble," she said. "Children move so fast, they get out of sight before we realize it."

The driver of the bulldozer, who said his name was Jim McCarty, was still a little shaky from his scare. But he did not act angry any longer. He said he was mighty glad he had been able to stop in time.

"I guess you children like to play around this place," he added. "Well, I'm afraid you won't be able to play here any longer."

"We have to come here," Freddie spoke up. "Our train's in the barn."

"Your train?" Jim repeated. He looked puzzled.

"Yes. Our Rootin' Tootin' Railroad," Freddie explained.

This made the man laugh. When the twins told

him about the wonderful gift Mr. Dodge had given them, Jim said he would knock off work for a little while and go look at it. His good humor returned, and by the time they all reached the barn, Flossie's narrow escape was forgotten.

Bert unlocked the doors, and proudly showed off the *Little Iron Horse* and the rest of the train.

Jim McCarty said, "You kids sure pulled a prize this time. My kids would love to own this," he added. "Maybe they can have a ride on it someday?"

"Sure," Bert replied. "But if we can't run our train here any longer, we'll have to find a new place. Our yard at home is too small. Do you know any place we could take it?"

"I'm afraid not," Jim replied. "But you'll have to find one in a hurry."

"Why?" Bert wanted to know.

Jim McCarty said the barn was going to be torn down in a few days! The news stunned Bert and the rest of the Bobbseys.

"That's very unfortunate," said Mrs. Bobbsey. "But I'll speak to my husband this evening about moving the train."

Jim went back to his work. The children discussed the sudden turn of events. How were they going to find a place for their little railroad in such a hurry?

"Maybe we'll have to store it in Dad's lumber-yard," said Bert with a sigh.

"That's no fun," Freddie groaned. "I want to ride on it."

There seemed to be no solution to the problem. Finally Nan suggested that they leave it to their father.

"While we're here," she said, "let's have a treasure hunt in the barn. Maybe we'll find some more clues."

Freddie was the first to find something, and ran to Mrs. Bobbsey with his *treasure*. It was the skeleton of a rat! His mother smiled weakly, pretending to like his find.

Bert dug up a battered-looking horse collar, which he declared had once hung around the neck of a proud trotter. Now, little stuffing was left in the collar. No doubt the rest had been carried off long ago by mice to build nests!

The amusing hunt went on for some time without any worthwhile objects being located. The twins were just tiring of the game, when Nan, who was in the haymow, gave an excited shriek.

"I've found a real treasure!" she cried, and came leaping down the ladder from the loft.

In her hand was a diamond ring—at least, the stone looked like a diamond as it sparkled in the sunshine. Mrs. Bobbsey examined it and said she was sure the stone was genuine.

"From the setting, I should say this ring was made

several years ago," she remarked. "I wonder if it belongs to Mrs. Dodge? I think we'd better stop at her apartment and find out."

Once more the barn was locked, and Mrs. Bobbsey drove directly to the Dodge home. Both Mr. and Mrs. Dodge were there and were amazed at Nan's discovery.

"It's a lovely old ring, but it doesn't belong to me," Mrs. Dodge said. "I wonder who could have dropped it in the haymow?"

Mr. Dodge said that so far as he could remember no woman had ever worked around the barn. "It's possible the ring was dropped in one of the fields and raked up with the hay," he guessed.

"Then it may have been in the barn a long time," his wife pointed out. "The mow hasn't been empty for years."

"That's true," said Mr. Dodge. "Well, this is a real mystery."

Suddenly Mrs. Dodge's eyes lighted up. "I just thought of something," she said. "Don't you remember, dear," she asked her husband, "the time that old tramp slept in our barn?"

Mr. Dodge said indeed he did. It was just about a year before, and the fellow had nearly set the place on fire with his pipe. It was very possible he had stolen the ring and had dropped it in the haymow.

Bert, too, had an idea. Maybe the man who had

been hiding in the barn and showered him and Charlie with hay had dropped the ring. He might even have been the same tramp.

"I'll bet he came back to look for the ring," Bert said.

"Maybe he stole the watch and was looking for that," Nan suggested.

"And maybe he took our tracks, too!" cried Freddie.

The grownups agreed that the children's reasoning was good. It did not solve the mystery, however. There was nothing to prove any connection between the ring and the watch. And nobody could be sure that the tramp had stolen some of the track of the Rootin' Tootin' Railroad.

"I'm afraid these mysteries that are popping up aren't going to be solved easily," said Mr. Dodge.

He was surprised to hear that the excavation work for the housing development had been started so soon. He had thought that the Bobbsey twins would be able to enjoy the little railroad at the farm for quite a while. He asked where they were going to move the train.

"We don't know," said Bert a bit sadly.

Mr. Dodge promised to let the Bobbseys know if he heard of any place where they might set up the little railroad. As they were about to leave, Mrs. Dodge handed the ring back to Nan. She said that since the farm no longer belonged to them, the ring did not either.

"Should I give it to the housing man?" Nan asked.

Mr. Dodge said that actually the barn would not belong to the housing man for a few days, until certain papers were signed.

"So the barn is still mine," he concluded, "and my wife and I can do whatever we wish to with the diamond ring."

Nan stared, unbelieving. Then she asked if this meant that—*finders keepers*—the ring would be hers if she could not locate the owner.

"I should say so," Mr. Dodge answered, his eyes twinkling.

CHAPTER XI

"DAD," said Freddie, when his father came home that evening, "we have to move the Rootin' Tootin' Railroad right away."

"Before dinner, my Fat Fireman?" Mr. Bobbsey grinned.

Flossie answered for her twin. "Maybe we'd better, 'cause the tramp's coming back for his ring, and he might take some more tracks, 'cause they're going to tear down the barn. The man that nearly ran over me said so."

"Whew!" Mr. Bobbsey laughed at his small daughter's complete story of the afternoon's happenings. Since he did not in the least understand what she meant, he said, "My Little Fat Fairy, suppose you start all over again and tell me the big news."

In a few minutes he had the story straight. He was sorry to hear the train would have to be moved from the farm.

"I can store it at the lumberyard only a short

75

time," he said. "Then, if we can't find another place for it, I'm afraid we'll have to give it away."

"We just *have* to find a place for it!" cried Flossie.

Bert and Nan were sure some kind of arrangement could be made. They would ask all their friends if they knew of a spot where the *Little Iron Horse* could go.

After supper they got busy on the telephone. Charlie, John, Nellie and Grace promised to ask their parents and let the Bobbseys know. They, too, wished the twins might keep their little railroad.

Flossie, in the meantime, had gone to the kitchen to talk to Sam. She asked him if there were any place where he delivered lumber for her daddy where the people would let them set up the Rootin' Tootin' Railroad. Sam could not think of any place at the moment, but there was one farm where it might be possible, he thought.

"The trouble is," he said, "that the farm's far out in the country and you all couldn't go there very often. You ought to have your railroad in a place that will be right easy to get to." Sam ran his fingers through his graying hair. "But I'll keep thinkin'," he promised.

The following morning Mr. Bobbsey said they should start moving the Rootin' Tootin' Railroad to his lumberyard. They would bring the tracks first.

Bert and Charlie went out to the Dodge farm with Sam to load the rails onto the truck. Both boys wished they might set up the railroad and run it once more, but the housing operations were almost up to the barn doors.

With a sigh, Bert looked at the engine and tender and passenger car, and then locked the doors. At the lumberyard the boys stored the tracks in a shed.

Bert and Charlie decided to remain at the yard awhile. A freighter had docked, and was getting ready to unload. Bert asked his father if the boys might stay around the rest of the morning, and help check the shipment of cedar planks.

"Glad to have your help," Mr. Bobbsey replied. "And how would you like to have lunch with me at Turner's restaurant, and work this afternoon?"

"I'd like to, sir," Charlie answered. Bert eagerly accepted also.

It was fun to watch the big crane on the freighter lift a stack of boards to the lumberyard dock. Then after the boys had written down just how many boards there were, Mr. Bobbsey's crane would pick them up and swing them to various parts of the lumberyard, and stack them into high, neat piles.

"It's too bad Freddie's not here," Bert remarked after lunch. "He's keen about riding in the cab of the crane."

At the moment Freddie was alone in the back yard

of his home, playing a game. He was a detective and he was hunting for the person who had taken the tracks of the Rootin' Tootin' Railroad. He had pretended the thief was hiding under bushes, under the porch, and finally in the garage. Now the little boy could not think of any more hiding places.

Just then Danny Rugg leaped the hedge and asked Freddie what the Bobbseys were going to do with the little railroad.

"I don't know," said Freddie.

"You won't be able to keep it," said Danny.

"Why not?" Freddie asked.

Danny smirked and said he knew a lot that Freddie did not know.

"I'm a detective," Freddie boasted. "I'll find out."

Danny asked more questions and soon Freddie had told him the whole story of the stolen tracks and how he was playing detective to catch the thief. He also told about the watch and the ring.

Danny was excited. He wanted to go look for treasures himself! And better yet he could play with the little railroad, and Bert Bobbsey could not stop him!

"Is the barn locked?" he asked.

"Uh-huh," Freddie answered.

Danny was not giving up. "I'll bet you know how to get in," he said.

"Sure I do," Freddie replied without thinking. "I know where there's a secret window."

He had had the wooden window pointed out to him, but did not know about the wedge Bert and Charlie had used to keep it from being opened.

Danny's brain was working fast. He must find some way to make Freddie show him where the secret window was. Finally a plan came to him.

"Say, Freddie," he said, "do you know where you'll probably find the man who took your tracks?"

"No, where?"

"Down by the real railroad tracks," said Danny. "I'll take you down there. I've got my bike. You can sit on the handle bars."

Freddie knew this was only part of the detective game, but it would be fun to go there. Knowing he should tell someone in the house where he was going, he raced up the back steps. No one was in the kitchen. Danny called that he could not wait. If Freddie was coming, he would have to hurry.

So Freddie hustled down the steps and out to the driveway. He climbed onto the handle bars and Danny pedaled off. He went very quickly, because he did not want to meet any of the Bobbsey family and have his little scheme spoiled.

When they reached the railroad track, Freddie hopped off. Seeing a shed, which held tools and lanterns, he sneaked up to it. The door was locked.

"Whoever is in there, come out!" he shouted.

No one opened the door. Freddie pounded on it. Danny stood in the background, grinning.

When he thought Freddie had played the game long enough, he said, "We're just too late, Freddie. The thief has gone back to the barn to steal some more stuff."

"Really?" Freddie asked. He was so deep in the spirit of the detective game that it did not occur to him that Danny was deliberately trying to get him to ride out to the old barn.

"Come on," Danny urged. "We'd better hurry or we won't catch the thief."

Once more Freddie climbed onto the handle bars and Danny started off. About halfway there, the little boy suddenly realized that Danny might play with the engine and damage it. He told Danny he wanted to go home.

"What?" said Danny. "And lose the thief?"

Freddie was quiet for a few minutes. When he asked once more to be taken home, Danny said slyly:

"Maybe we'll find another watch or a ring in the barn. If I find anything, I'll go halves with you."

"Okay," Freddie agreed.

When they reached the Dodge farm, Danny was grinning. He had put one over on Bert Bobbsey!

"Where's the window?" he asked Freddie as he leaned his bicycle against the barn.

The little boy pointed. Danny walked over to it, reached up, and tried to open the window. But the wooden panel would not budge.

Danny was angry. "It's locked!" he cried. "Tell me how to get into this barn, Freddie Bobbsey, or you'll be sorry!"

Freddie was frightened. There had been other times in his life when Danny Rugg had carried out similar threats. There was no telling what the big boy might do to him now!

CHAPTER XII

LOST AND FOUND

DANNY RUGG stood glaring at little Freddie Bobbsey, who was too frightened to speak.

"Why didn't you tell me the window was locked?" Danny demanded.

"I-I didn't know," Freddie managed to stammer.

"I'll fix you for this!" the older boy cried.

As he paused to think up some way to get even, Freddie's courage returned. Actually he was glad that Danny Rugg could not get into the barn and perhaps damage the *Little Iron Horse*. He tried to get Danny's mind off the barn by pointing out the housing development work that was going on.

"Let's go watch the bulldozer," he said, starting away.

Danny was not ready to give up, but he followed the little boy. They watched Jim McCarty for a while, but he said it was against the rules to offer rides. Anyway, it was nearly quitting time.

Danny said he was going off to look at the Dodge

82

house. He did not wait for Freddie, and by the time the small boy reached the house, Danny was out of sight.

"Where are you?" Freddie called loudly.

There was no answer. Freddie ran all the way around the big house. Still there was no sign of the older boy.

"I guess he went back to the barn," thought Freddie, and skipped off.

But Danny was not there, either. What was even worse, his bicycle was gone!

"He's gone home without me!" Freddie wailed. Jim McCarty and the other workmen had quit for the day. No one was around.

At that moment Freddie spied someone on a bicycle at the far end of the field where the bulldozer had been working. The little boy yelled loudly and ran toward it. He was not halfway there when the bicycle and its rider disappeared in a woods.

Reaching the woods, Freddie dashed in among the trees, and called again. This time he thought he heard someone say, "Hello!"

Freddie ran in the direction of the sound. Still he saw nobody, and decided to go back. But he was deep in the woods now, with no idea which way to go to get back to the barn. Tears came to his eyes. He tried to think what Bert or his daddy might do if they were lost in the woods.

"They would look for their footprints," decided Detective Freddie.

After looking around a few minutes, he found two marks of his own shoes. Encouraged, he hunted for more. But the ground was hard and there were many leaves lying on it, so it was difficult for Freddie to find the places where he had stepped.

He kept on searching until it started to grow dark. Freddie knew now that he was lost, and he was tired and hungry. It was all Danny Rugg's fault.

"When I get home, I'm going—I'm going to punch Danny Rugg as hard as I can," he told himself. "And I'll get Bert to fight him, too!"

In the meantime, Danny Rugg had become very much worried. He had only planned to play a little trick on Freddie and give him a scare. He had found a way to get into the Dodge house and was hiding inside while Freddie was looking for him.

When Danny got back to the barn, Freddie was gone and so was Danny's bicycle. Knowing Freddie was too little to ride it, he wondered who had taken it. Maybe Bert Bobbsey had come and ridden his small brother home.

As Danny thought about this, he became very angry and decided to go directly to the Bobbsey home and have it out with Bert. But by the time he had trudged along the road twenty minutes, he changed his mind. Suppose somebody *else* had taken his bicycle! Suppose Freddie was still out at the farm alone, maybe lost in the woods!

Reaching a grocery store at the side of the road, Danny went inside to telephone. He called the Bobbsey home. Bert answered.

Danny tried to disguise his voice and make it sound like a younger boy's. "Is Freddie there?" he asked.

"No. Who is this?"

Danny did not answer the question. He began to shake with fright. He knew now that Freddie's family had not found out where Freddie was, so Bert could not have taken the bicycle. Danny hung up hurriedly.

"Then who did take my bike?" Danny thought as he went outside. His father would be angry about the bicycle, he knew.

As the boy walked along, he made a sudden decision. He would go to his grandmother and ask her to help him. But when his grandmother heard the story, she was shocked and said:

"Danny, we must go right over to the Bobbsey home and tell them everything."

"But that won't get my bicycle back," the boy objected.

"That makes no difference," she said. "Something may happen to Freddie Bobbsey."

When they reached the twins' home, they found

the Bobbsey family greatly excited. They had called several of Freddie's friends, but there had been no report about Freddie.

Danny was too nervous to talk, so his grandmother told the story. As soon as Mr. Bobbsey heard it, he telephoned the police and asked them to start a search at once at the Dodge farm. He would follow in his car.

"Please, Daddy, please," Flossie begged, as he got ready to leave. "I-I-want to go find Freddie, too. He's my twin."

In the end all the children and their mother went along. Danny's grandmother left them, but said Danny should go to help find Freddie.

When they reached the farm, armed with flashlights, a police car was just pulling in. Two policemen got out and spoke to Mr. Bobbsey.

While they were talking, Bert picked up the bicycle tracks with his flashlight. "Let's follow these!" he urged. "Come on, Danny! Maybe the thief took Freddie off on the handle bars!"

Bert dashed ahead with Danny at his heels. Little Flossie went after them, but she could not keep up with them and came running back.

One of the officers suggested that if the Bobbseys wanted to help search, it would be best for the group to separate. He directed that Mr. Bobbsey look in and around the old barn, with perhaps Mrs. Bobbsey and Flossie helping. He himself would go after the boys, who already had entered the woods. The other policeman would search the house.

After the others had gone, Nan realized that she had not been given any job. Left to herself, she decided to look in the old well, but found it safely covered. Next she crossed the plowed field to the pond where Flossie's doll Marie had fallen in. To her relief, Freddie was not there.

Nan looked around, wondering where else to search. She decided upon the woods, and set off, following a different direction from the one the boys had taken.

Nan knew she should not walk in the woods without looking around carefully and marking spots so that she could find her way back. Where she entered, there was a tall oak with a large hollowed-out spot in one side of the trunk. She would remember this.

Beaming her flashlight, she walked several yards, then stopped. A clump of bushes with red berries on them became her second landmark. As she went on a few more yards, Nan began calling loudly:

"Freddie! Freddie! If you can hear me, answer!"

Were her ears deceiving her, or did she hear a faint voice far off? Again she called. This time she was sure she was not mistaken. A thin little voice said:

"I'm over here where the frogs live!"

Nan hurried forward, forgetting to note land-marks in her speed to reach Freddie. She flashed her light around, and finally it revealed Freddie. He was sitting on the ground, his back against a tree.

In front of him was a little pool. Sitting round its edges were several frogs which seemed to be tame. But as Nan ran up, the frogs splashed into the water.

"You scared 'em!" Freddie pouted. He seemed to have forgotten that he was lost, and of course he did not know that not only his own family but many other people and the police were very much worried about him.

"Are you all right?" Nan asked him, kneeling on the ground beside her small brother.

"Course I'm all right," Freddie answered.

He told about following the bicycle and getting lost. He said he had planned to stay in the woods all night with the nice frogs.

"But let's go home. I'm hungry," he said.

The two children hurried off. Nan thought she knew exactly where she was going, but suddenly she realized nothing looked familiar.

"Hello! Hello!" she cried out.

"What's the matter?" asked Freddie.

Nan did not want to tell him she thought they were lost. "Follow me," she said.

A moment later Nan grabbed Freddie's hand. She was sure she had heard a noise that sounded like someone snoring. Nan flashed her light around and then gasped.

Not far to their left, a man lay asleep on the ground. Alongside a tree stood a bicycle. Was it Danny's, and was the sleeping man the person who had taken it, the children wondered?

CHAPTER XIII

DINAH'S STRANGE STORY

IT WAS several seconds before Nan Bobbsey could make up her mind what to do. Here was someone who might show her and Freddie how to get out of the woods. Yet caution told her she should not disturb the man, especially if he was the one who had taken Danny's bicycle.

Nan leaned down and whispered to Freddie that they should hurry along as quietly as possible and not disturb the man. The police would take care of him.

As the children tiptoed off, Nan again wondered which way to go. Then out of the darkness not far ahead she saw a light gleaming. Relieved, she set off in that direction.

"There they are!" Freddie shouted loudly, as he and Nan walked out of the woods.

"Shh!" his sister cautioned him. She did not want the sleeping man to be awakened and get away before a policeman could talk to him.

From across the field, several flashlights came toward them. Presently Mr. and Mrs. Bobbsey and Flossie reached Freddie and Nan.

"Freddie! Freddie!" his mother cried, hugging her small son tightly. "Where have you been?"

Freddie told his story again. Then his father asked whether he and Nan had seen Bert and Danny.

"No, Dad," Nan replied. "And they didn't answer when I was calling Freddie."

"That's funny," said Mr. Bobbsey. "I wonder where they went."

At this moment the policeman who had been searching the house ran up. He was relieved to see Freddie, and said he would summon the others over the loudspeaker in his car.

"Oh, officer," said Nan, "please don't do that until you talk to the man with the bicycle."

"What do you mean?" the policeman asked.

Nan told him about the sleeping man, and the officer asked her to point out the place where she had seen him.

"I'll try to find it," Nan said, and led the way back into the woods. Mr. Bobbsey went along, but the others returned to the barn.

"I'm sure it was somewhere around here," Nan whispered a few minutes later.

She circled her flashlight among some trees which looked familiar. Yes, there lay the man!

"Wait here!" the officer ordered the others. He walked over to the man, leaned down, and shook him.

"Wh-wh-what's the matter?" the fellow asked sleepily, sitting up and rubbing his eyes.

"What's your name?" the officer asked him.

"Why, it's—it's John Blaine."

"Where did you get this bicycle?"

The man yawned and said, "What bicycle?"

The policeman pointed to the one standing near the tree. Suddenly the man became wide awake, as he noticed the other's uniform. He jumped up and dashed toward the bicycle.

"Hold on there!" the policeman said, grabbing hold of the small, thin man's shoulder. "I asked you where you got the bicycle."

"That's my business," the fellow snapped. "It belongs to me."

The trooper beckoned toward Nan and her father. "Will you come here, please?" he asked. As Nan appeared, he said, "Would you recognize Danny Rugg's bicycle?"

"Yes," Nan said.

Nan had seen Danny's bicycle many times. It was a black and red one. This bicycle was black and red. And the front wheel was a little crooked, like the one on Danny's bicycle.

"I'm sure this is it," said Nan.

"I guess you're guilty of stealing the bicycle," the officer told the fellow. He had been holding his arm tightly. "Come along with me."

"I ain't done nothin'," the stranger protested. "You can't arrest me."

He had hardly said this when the other policeman and two boys came rushing through the underbrush toward them. The boys were Bert and Danny, who were glad to hear that Freddie was safe.

"And you got my bike back!" Danny cried gleefully.

The officer holding the prisoner looked at Danny. "Yes," he said severely, "but I think it should be taken away from you until you can behave yourself better."

"Oh, please, please, don't take my bike away from me," Danny pleaded. "I—I need it for school and—and to go on errands for my mother. Please don't take it away."

The policeman said he would take both Danny and the bicycle home and talk the matter over with his father. Then the two officers hustled the prisoner into their car and started back to town.

Mr. Bobbsey took his family home to a late supper. Dinah and Sam had to hear Freddie's story. When he got to the part about the frogs, Freddie suggested that he go back to the pool the next day and get some of them to bring home.

"My gracious sakes!" Dinah exclaimed. "Where would we put a lot of frogs?"

Freddie thought maybe they could build a pond in the back yard. It was not until Sam assured him the frogs would not stay there long, that Freddie gave up the idea.

Early next morning a telephone call came for Mr. Bobbsey. It was from the president of the company working on the housing development. He said the miniature railroad would have to be moved very soon. The barn was to be torn down in two days.

"All right," Mr. Bobbsey agreed, but to his family he said, "I just don't know how I'm going to spare the time or the space either. I have a new shipment of lumber coming in tomorrow and it'll fill the yard up."

"Dad!" Nan said excitedly. "I know a place where we might take our *Little Iron Horse!*"

"Where?"

"To the vacant lot alongside the Powers'," his daughter replied. "It's very large."

"Sure," said Bert. "It's big enough to set up the railroad."

"And maybe Mr. Power would watch it for us," Nan added.

Eagerly the children dashed from the house to go and ask the Powers who the owner of the next-door lot was. They found the young man and his mother sitting on their front porch.

"Why, that lot belongs to us," said Mrs. Power. "We've had it up for sale a long time, but haven't been able to sell it. I think it would be a fine place for your miniature railroad. We'll be very glad to watch it, won't we, Clinton?"

Her son said indeed he would. And he thought it might be best to keep the engine and the passenger car under a little shed at the far end of the property, in case of rain.

"Oh, that's just scrumptious!" said Flossie. "You're the nicest people in all this town."

The Powers laughed and said they were very glad to help out such nice children. When would they like to bring the railroad?

"Right away," Bert replied. "The housing people want to tear down the barn in two days."

"Bring it any time," said Clinton Power.

The twins raced home to tell the good news. To their amazement the kitchen door was locked. Dinah unlocked it and let them in. She looked very much excited.

"What's the matter?" Nan asked.

"Yes," said Bert. "why was the door locked?"

"Oh, somethin' awful happened while you all were away," Dinah answered. "A man tried to come right into my kitchen, and said I had to give him that diamond ring you found, Nan!"

CHAPTER XIV

NAN'S SCARE

DINAH was so excited that she could hardly tell the story. Waving her hands, she cried:

"He kept tryin' to get in the house!"

"Where was Mother?" Bert asked.

"She went out right after you all did," the cook replied. "She got a phone call to hurry over to Redfield. Some lady there is real sick."

The twins did not know anyone in Redfield, and they wondered who the person might be. Perhaps it was a club friend of their mother's.

"Tell us some more about the bad man," Flossie begged.

"It's a good thing I'm a big woman," said Dinah, rolling her eyes. "I was just as strong as that awful man—maybe stronger. When he pushed himself into my kitchen, I just pushed him right back out again."

"Good for you!" cried Freddie. "I hope you pushed him good and hard. Did he fall down?"

Dinah said she had not shoved the stranger that hard; only hard enough to get him outside.

"And I said to him, 'Get yourself away from here and don't you never come back, 'cause old Dinah ain't givin' away any diamond rings to strangers.' Then I slammed the door and locked it!"

The younger twins laughed and praised their faithful cook again. But Nan and Bert were quiet. How did the man know about the diamond ring? Was he the tramp Mr. Dodge thought had stolen the ring and dropped it in the barn?

"We'll sure keep the doors to this house locked from now on," Bert declared.

That afternoon it seemed as if Freddie and Flossie wanted to run in and out of the house more than they had ever done before. Poor Dinah was kept busy answering the bell until she was nearly frantic.

"I declare to goodness," she said, "if this keeps up, I'll have to give you children a key."

This pleased Freddie immensely. He begged to have one immediately. Dinah found an extra key to the back door and handed it to him.

"Take good care of it," she said.

He promised he would and skipped outside with Flossie.

"Let's play I'm that bad man," Freddie suggested. "You go inside and be Dinah. I'll come in and take your diamond ring away from you."

A few minutes later Freddie let himself into the kitchen.

"I want your diamond ring!" he demanded of Flossie.

"You can't have it," she said. Then to Freddie's surprise, she let Waggo out of the pantry where she had hidden him, and said, "Sic 'im! Chase that bad man!"

Dinah laughed. She had not thought of getting Waggo to help her!

Flossie and Freddie played various games, using the key, until Mr. Bobbsey arrived home. When he heard about the man demanding the ring, he became concerned, and asked Dinah for more details about him.

She said the man was of middle age, short, rather stout, and had a scar on the back of his right hand. Mr. Bobbsey telephoned the police and gave them the description. The captain promised to hunt for the fellow.

"If he shows up at your house again, have someone call us at once," the captain requested.

Mr. Bobbsey repeated this message to Dinah and the children. Then he asked where Mrs. Bobbsey was. Hearing that she had gone to Redfield early that morning, the twins' father frowned. He had never heard his wife mention having any friend in Redfield.

"Did she say when she'd be back, Dinah?" he asked.

"No sir, she didn't."

The family waited half an hour for her, then Mr. Bobbsey told Dinah to serve supper. He kept wondering why his wife did not telephone. The family were just finishing their dessert when she came in.

Flossie hopped up to hug her mother. "Was the lady awful sick?" she asked.

"No one was sick," Mrs. Bobbsey replied. "I've been on a wild-goose chase."

After she had kissed each member of her family, she said that apparently the telephone call to her had been some kind of a joke. She could not understand, though, why anyone should play such an unkind trick on her.

"You think someone just pretended to be a friend of yours and asked you to go all the way to Redfield?" her husband exclaimed.

"That's right," Mrs. Bobbsey answered. "A man telephoned here, saying he was the husband of my friend Mrs. Thatcher. He told me she was in the Redfield hospital and had asked that I come to see her."

Mrs. Bobbsey went on to say that when she arrived at the large Redfield hospital, Mrs. Thatcher was not there. Learning of two other small hospitals in town, the twins' mother had gone to each of them.

It was not until she learned her friend was not at any of them, that she had become suspicious and telephoned the Thatcher house. Her friend was home and perfectly well!

"Who do you suppose the man was who phoned?" Mrs. Bobbsey asked.

"It was that bad man—the one who came here to steal Nan's diamond ring!" said Flossie.

Mrs. Bobbsey was amazed when she heard what had happened, and agreed that the telephone call must have come from the man with the scar on his right hand. He wanted to make sure nobody would be at home but Dinah.

"But thanks to you, Dinah, his trick didn't work," said Mrs. Bobbsey. Then she became thoughtful. "I wonder how he knew Mrs. Thatcher is my friend?"

"Easy enough," her husband suggested. "The newspaper had a story about your club. It mentioned both you and Mrs. Thatcher."

After the excitement had died down, Bert recalled that his parents did not know about the offer of the Powers to have the miniature railroad set up on their lot. Mr. and Mrs. Bobbsey were pleased to hear this. Mr. Bobbsey said he would insist upon renting the property.

"I'll call on Mr. Power tomorrow to make the arrangements," he added. "But the train can't be moved for a while yet. All of the trucks will be busy."

"But Dad," Bert said, "they're going to tear down the barn on Friday."

"I've taken care of the matter," his father assured him. "They've put it off until Tuesday."

Next morning Mrs. Bobbsey told Freddie and Flossie that she was going to take them shopping for some new playclothes. Later they would have lunch in town with Daddy.

Soon after they had left, Dinah went to the laundry in the basement and started washing. Bert decided to sew up a ripped baseball mitt before having a catch with Charlie. While he was working on it, Nan sat down at the piano to practice.

Presently the doorbell rang and Nan went to answer it. On the porch stood two men. One of them was short and rather stout. The other wore a policeman's uniform.

"Are you Nan Bobbsey?" the policeman asked.

"Yes."

Bert came into the hall. "Is something wrong?" he asked.

"I want that diamond ring!" the stout man said in a gruff voice, pushing his way into the hall. "You give it to me at once, Nan Bobbsey, or this policeman will arrest you."

Nan was frightened. She did not want to give up

the ring, but if the police thought she should, it must be all right.

"I'll get it," she said, and started up the stairway.

Bert stared hard at the man who had asked for the ring. He did not like his looks. Maybe he was the same one who had come before. The man had his right hand in his pocket, so Bert could not see whether or not there was a scar on it.

The policeman acted strangely, too. Bert had a feeling Nan should not give the ring to them.

He followed his twin upstairs, and whispered that he would go down the back stairs and speak to Dinah about it. He would ask her to see if the stout, gruff man was the one who had been there the day before.

"Listen," he said to his twin, "make out you can't find the ring. Stall 'em a little while!"

Nan said she would try her best. She wondered how long she could put the men off.

Bert quickly disappeared down the back stairway. Upon reaching the basement, he told Dinah what was happening upstairs. Dinah threw up her hands.

"Lawsy me!" she exclaimed. "This is terrible! I don't trust those men nohow. Bert, you sneak out the cellar door and go over to Mis' Smith's and call the police. Hurry back as fast as you can!"

Bert unlocked the basement door, and ran across the yard to the neighbor's house. As Dinah started up the stairway, she heard the gruff man shout:

"Hurry up with that ring! I can't wait here all day!"

Poor Nan did not know what to do. Bert had not come back to tell her what Dinah had said. She picked up the diamond ring and walked out to the hall.

"Make it snappy!" the man demanded.

"Yeh," the policeman added, "bring that ring here, or I'll take you off to jail."

The gruff man did not wait for Nan to reach the foot of the stairs. He rushed up to meet her, and grabbed the ring just as Dinah ran into the hall.

"You leave that ring be!" the cook cried.

She tried to take it away from him, but she was no match for the two men. The one in uniform opened the front door, and both men bolted from the house.

CHAPTER XV

THE JUGGLERS

BERT dashed across the lawn after the fleeing men. The police captain had told him that no officer had gone to the Bobbsey home. Both of these men were thieves, Bert was sure.

"Stop!" he shouted as they jumped into a car, slammed the door, and roared off.

At that moment a police car drove around the corner. Bert hurried to it, with Nan and Dinah following.

"What's the matter, boy?" the driver asked. "I picked up an urgent radio message to hurry here."

Bert quickly told what had happened. "There they go now!" he shouted, pointing far down the street.

"Hop in, fellow," the officer commanded. "You two better not come," he advised Nan and Dinah.

Bert and the policeman sped after the thieves, siren wailing. People turned to stare at the chase.

At the edge of town the radio car caught up to

105

the thieves' automobile and forced it to the curb. As it screeched to a stop, the right-hand door was flung open and the two men leaped out.

The patrolman went for the man in the uniform. Bert dashed after the one who had snatched the ring.

"Give me back that ring!" he shouted.

The fellow paid no attention. He ran down a driveway and leaped a back fence. But Bert was catching up now. As the boy vaulted the fence, he could hear the stout man puffing. They raced into an open field. As Bert was about to overtake him, the man stopped and faced the boy.

"Take your ring!" he shouted. "And leave me alone!"

He flung the ring a distance behind Bert. By the time he located it, the thief had disappeared.

Bert returned to the police car, which now was surrounded by a crowd of people. The patrolman had put handcuffs on the man in uniform, saying he was not a real officer at all.

"I was only going to a masquerade party," the thief kept saying, and everybody laughed.

"Tell it to the captain," the radio policeman said. Then he turned to Bert. "Where's the other man?"

The boy told of his escape. Then he showed the officer the ring.

"Good work," the policeman said. "I'll drive you home and then take care of this man."

Bert was met in front of the Bobbsey house by Nan and Dinah, who were amazed to learn that he had gotten the ring back.

"You're a mighty clever young detective," Dinah praised him.

"But *you* told me to call the police," Bert grinned.

Suddenly Nan had an idea. "Bert," she said, "that man who took the ring looked very familiar."

"You mean you know who he is?" Bert asked excitedly.

"N-n-no," Nan answered slowly. "But I'm sure I've seen him some place. I wish I could remember—"

When Mr. Bobbsey came home that evening and heard about the latest happenings, he sighed and then chuckled.

"My goodness," he said, "this house is as busy as a railroad station. Every night you have some new excitement to tell me. I hope these mysteries will be solved soon."

Then he announced that he was going to take the twins to a little show the next day.

"Where is it?" Freddie asked.

"In Claremont. I have business to attend to there. The man I'm going to see suggested I bring you children to see the entertainment."

Mr. Bobbsey said that one of the Sunday Schools in Claremont was having an outing. A committee had arranged little side shows for the children who were to come.

"What kind of shows?" Bert asked.

Mr. Bobbsey said he had been told there was to be a clown who was very good at doing tricks.

"Oh, I want to see him," said Flossie. "I wish tomorrow would hurry up and come."

"It'll come sooner if you go to bed early," laughed Mrs. Bobbsey, and Flossie went upstairs at once.

Mr. Bobbsey and the twins arrived early at the grounds where the outing would take place. He warned Bert and Nan to take good care of their brother and sister, and handed each of them a box of lunch. Then he drove off.

"I'm hungry," Freddie announced.

"Let's look around a little before we eat," Nan suggested. "See all those little tents over there. I'll bet they're the side shows."

Not many people had come yet to the outing, and the clown Mr. Bobbsey had mentioned was not ready for his act. When the four children showed up, however, he said he would do a few of his tricks for them. He called out:

"Jackie! Come, son! We have some visitors!"

A boy about Bert's age walked from behind a curtain. He was dressed in a tight-fitting red suit, but he was not made up like a clown as his father was.

One could hardly tell what the father really looked like, because of his funny costume. He wore a large white suit with balloon trousers. A pointed hat was perched on one side of his head. He had a large false nose, and his face was painted to make him look as if he were grinning all the time.

"Here I go," said his son.

He reached under the counter, took out several colored balls, and began to juggle them. The Bobbseys thought it was wonderful the way the boy could keep seven different balls in the air all at once, and not drop one of them.

"Watch out, Pop!" he exclaimed.

He bounced one of the balls right onto his father's nose!

"Oh!" cried Flossie, expecting the nose to fall off. But instead the clown balanced the ball neatly on it.

The boy juggled the balls a few more seconds, then suddenly threw one to the top of the clown's head. As he sent the ball back, another one landed on his neck, another on his shoulder, another on his back. All the balls were bouncing back and forth, from the boy to the clown, in perfect rhythm!

"Gee, that's swell," Bert cried enthusiastically.

Freddie climbed to the counter of the little booth. He was just about to drop down inside, and ask the boy to show him how to juggle the balls, when the clown picked him up. He tossed him into the air, and Freddie suddenly found himself sitting on the clown's shoulders!

The little boy was very much surprised, but he liked the trick and grinned from ear to ear. Then he got down.

"What's your name?" Flossie asked the clown's son.

"Jackie Braun."

"Where do you live?"

"Oh, I don't live anywhere special," the boy answered.

"Not anywhere!" Flossie repeated. "You mean you have no home?"

The boy answered he had sort of a traveling home. He and his father lived in a trailer and they went from town to town all over the country, giving their show.

At that moment they heard a shout behind them, and saw a group of children coming in a bus.

"Let's go over and see if we know any of them," Nan suggested.

She thanked the clown and Jackie for the show, and said they would come back after lunch to watch them perform. The Bobbseys did not know any of the children in the bus, but they found them very friendly, and played games with them until lunchtime.

After everyone had eaten, a man announced through a megaphone that there would be a show for the children in the big tent. If they would walk over there and take seats, the show would begin in about ten minutes.

"Let's go!" Freddie urged.

The four Bobbseys followed the other children to a large tent, and took seats together about halfway down. Soon the curtain went up and a man came out with a big, black hat.

"You see there is nothing in here," he said, turning the inside of the hat toward the audience. Sure enough, it was empty.

He now turned the hat around, reached down inside, and began taking small paper boxes out of it. Would he never stop! Soon he had a whole pile of them alongside him.

"My goodness!" he exclaimed. "Did you children throw these boxes in here?"

As the audience laughed, the magician began to throw the boxes out toward the children. Flossie caught one of them.

"There's a surprise inside each one," the man called out.

The children who had caught the boxes hurriedly opened them. Inside Flossie's was a little toy dog. She declared it looked exactly like Waggo!

The show lasted nearly an hour. When it was

over, the twins went outside. Flossie and Freddie wanted to see the clown and his son again, so the four children walked back.

Nan suddenly grabbed Bert's arm. "Look!" she cried. "There goes that dreadful man who tried to steal my diamond ring!"

CHAPTER XVI

FIREMAN FREDDIE

"WHERE?" Bert cried, looking around hurriedly.

"Over there!" Nan pointed to a group of people walking toward a tent.

"I'll get him!" Bert declared. "You watch Freddie and Flossie."

He dashed off and looked everywhere for the man, but could not find him. When Nan and the small twins caught up to Bert, he said he was going to telephone to Detective Lynch and let him know about the thief. He asked a woman where he might find a telephone, and was directed to a house down the road.

"We'll meet you at Jackie Braun's booth," said Nan.

They walked over to it. Mr. Braun and his son were doing a new act. The clown had started a cane twirling on the end of one finger. Now he gave it a shove into the air. The cane landed on one of Jackie's fingers and kept right on twirling!

113

"Gee, I'd like to try that," said Freddie. "I'm going to get the old cane in our hall closet soon as I get home, and do that trick."

Nan smiled. "I bet it takes years of practice to learn how to do that trick," she said.

"But Jackie isn't very old," said Freddie. "I bet I could learn it in just about one week."

In ten minutes Bert returned. With him was Mr. Bobbsey, who said he had been looking everywhere for his children. In the excitement the twins had forgotten all about him!

"I think we'd better go home now," he said. "You've seen everything here, haven't you?"

"Yes," Freddie answered. "But Jackie's the best of all."

The twins introduced their father to the Brauns, and he watched their juggling act a few minutes.

"They're certainly clever," he said. "And very nice people, too."

On the way home, Freddie told his father he wanted to learn the cane trick and asked if he might use the cane which had belonged to the twins' grand-father.

"I'm afraid that's too heavy for you to hold on the end of your finger," Mr. Bobbsey said. "But I'll tell you where we might get a light cane."

"You mean buy one?" Freddie asked eagerly.

"Exactly," his father replied. Then he added

mysteriously, "We can probably pick one up when we go to the fair."

"Fair?" the four children asked together.

Their father said there was to be a County Firemen's Fair in Claremont very soon. All the surrounding towns, including Lakeport, were taking part. There would be many things for sale. Part of the proceeds would go to charity, part to the people selling them.

"Will there be games to play?" Flossie asked, "and things to ride on?"

Her father said there would be many amusements and the children ought to have a lot of fun. There would be a merry-go-round, a Ferris wheel, a little roller coaster and pony rides.

Nan went to bed that night full of thoughts about the Firemen's Fair. When she opened her eyes next morning an idea came to her. She was so excited about it that she quickly put on her robe and slippers and ran to tell her mother.

"Good morning, dear," said Mrs. Bobbsey, who was just going downstairs. "You look excited. What is it?"

"Mother, what would you think of Mrs. Power selling some of her old toys at the Firemen's Fair? Part would be for charity and she could keep the rest."

Mrs. Bobbsey said she liked the idea, but she wondered if Mrs. Power would want to sell her heir-looms.

"Why don't you ask her?" she suggested.

Immediately after breakfast Nan went to see Mrs. Power. She was delighted with the plan, but would the firemen want to do it, she wondered.

"I don't know anyone to consult about it," she remarked.

Nan said she knew the men at the firehouse near the Bobbsey home. Freddie loved to go there, and because of this, all the twins often stopped in.

"I'll ask them if you want me to," Nan offered eagerly.

"Please do," said Mrs. Power.

Nan had to pass her own home on the way to the firehouse, so she took Freddie with her. He was thrilled.

As soon as they reached the firehouse, he went off to inspect a wonderful new red and white engine that he had not seen before. A friendly fireman showed him all the gadgets and even let him ring the bell softly. Freddie climbed in and out of the truck just like a real fireman.

In the meantime, Nan had found out that one of the men was on the committee for the fair. She explained her plan to him about Mrs. Power selling toys.

"Do you think it would be all right?" she asked.

The man looked down at Nan's bright face. He liked the Bobbsey family very much. They were always doing something to help people less fortunate than themselves.

"I don't see why not," he smiled. "We'll set aside a special booth for Mrs. Power's toys."

Nan was eager to hurry back to Mrs. Power and tell her the good news. She thanked the fireman, and then looked around for her brother. Freddie was not in sight. She called him, but there was no answer.

"Oh dear," said Nan. "Where can he be? I want to hurry."

Freddie was found at last by one of the firemen. He had gone up the spiral stairway to see the firemen's beds, and even to lie down upon one of them a few seconds.

"I'm doing everything real firemen do," he explained.

"Your sister wants you," the man said.

"Okay. Here I go!"

With that Freddie jumped toward the shiny pole which the firemen slid down when they were in a hurry, instead of using the stairway.

"Don't!" the man cried.

It was too late. ZIP! Down went Freddie!

"Oh!" cried Nan, as she saw him coming down. But Freddie landed safely.

When Nan told him they must leave now and go to Mrs. Power's house, Freddie did not want to go. He was having too good a time.

"Please, Nan, let me stay here," he begged. "I'll go home real soon. Please!"

"All right," said Nan. "But be good and don't slide down that pole again!"

Freddie promised. He watched the men polish the new engine a few minutes. Then he disappeared.

The firemen thought he had gone home, but Freddie had climbed into the hook and ladder. It was the latest type and the ladder fascinated him. When it opened at a fire, it seemed to grow, section by section.

"I wish there'd be a fire," the little boy said to himself, as he crawled along one of the ladders. Presently he went down deeper into the truck and soon was completely out of sight.

Within fifteen seconds Freddie's wish came true. The telephone rang, then the gong in the firehouse. All the men left their work and jumped onto the fire engine and the hook and ladder. Within two seconds they were on the street, the bells clanging, the sirens shrieking.

Freddie Bobbsey had never been more thrilled in his life!

CHAPTER XVII

FUN IN AN ATTIC

WH-R-R-R-R-R-R!

Freddie Bobbsey held his hands tightly over his ears as the siren on the hook and ladder screeched. The noise seemed to go right through his head. But he loved the fast ride.

"I hope it's a big fire," he thought excitedly.

As they turned a corner and rushed down another street, he wondered how far away the fire was. Freddie was so deep in the truck, he could not see anything on the street. He was clinging to one rung of the ladder, with his feet wound tightly around another rung. This was the only way he could keep from bumping his head.

The big truck stopped with a sudden jerk, which nearly threw Freddie off his perch. Then he heard one of the firemen say:

"This looks like a bad one!"

Freddie realized that he should get off the fire

truck. Any minute the men would want to use the ladder. The little boy started climbing up through the bars of the various sections. He had just reached the rungs of the topmost section when the ladder began to move up.

It was too late for Freddie to get down. He hung on with all his strength. Higher and higher into the air he went!

"Hey! Look at that!" one of the firemen shouted, spotting the little boy.

The man jumped off the truck and raced around to the driver, who controlled the machinery that raised the ladder into the air.

The ladder moved swiftly. A moment later it straightened out and the second section began rising from the truck. Freddie looked down. The street seemed a long way below him. He became a little dizzy.

"Hold that ladder!" the fireman cried to the driver.

Hearing the command, the man stopped the machinery instantly. But by this time Freddie was opposite a second-floor window. A great billow of smoke came directly toward him! He coughed and nearly lost his grip on the ladder.

Another fireman ran up the rungs toward him. "Hang on till I get there!" he shouted.

Freddie tried to hold his breath to keep from

swallowing the smoke. He felt faint—he could not hold on any longer!

The next thing the little boy knew, he was lying face down on the sidewalk, and someone was rubbing his back.

"You all right?" a fireman's voice asked.

Freddie turned himself over and sat up. For a second he could not remember what had happened. Then he saw the fire engine and the hook and ladder. He felt very much ashamed and began to cry.

"That's all right, little man," said the fireman, helping him to his feet. "You weren't hurt."

"I know I wasn't," Freddie sobbed, "but I always wanted to be a fireman. Then when I got to be a fireman, I didn't know how to eat the smoke!"

"Well, real firemen don't either," the man said.

There was an abrupt movement in the crowd, and Nan Bobbsey pushed her way through.

"Oh, Freddie!" she cried. "I was so worried about you. When I heard the engines, I ran back to the firehouse, but you had gone. What happened?"

Freddie shook his head, but said nothing. He hated to tell his sister he had nearly been overcome by the smoke.

"Let's watch the fire," he said, and started walking closer to the pumper.

A policeman held the children back, for the fire was a bad one, and he did not want them getting into trouble. Nan thought Freddie should go home as he looked pale, but he begged to stay a few minutes longer.

A fireman wearing a smoke mask was just coming down the ladder holding a dog. The poor animal was quite limp, and the children hoped the rescue squad would be able to revive him.

"We can't go now," said Freddie. "We have to wait and see if the dog gets well."

The children could not see the dog after it reached the ground, but a few minutes later they asked a policeman about it. He said the little pup was all right.

"I guess you'd call him a hero dog," the officer said. "He was the only one in the apartment where the fire was. When the fire started, he barked loudly, and one of the neighbors came and saw the smoke."

"How wonderful!" said Nan.

She told Freddie that there were no more people to rescue, and they really must go home. Freddie left reluctantly, but he did feel rather ill now, so he did not protest any longer. When they reached the house, Mrs. Bobbsey, amazed at her small son's adventure, insisted that Freddie go to bed.

Flossie fluttered around her twin, wide-eyed. Every time she thought about what might have happened to him, she shivered a little.

"I don't ever want to be a fire lady when I grow

up," she said. "I want to make dolls—dolls with pretty faces—dolls with pretty clothes."

Nan said that she would like that better, too. She wondered if Mrs. Power had some pretty dolls in her collection of old toys which she might be willing to sell at the Firemen's Fair. They ought to bring a high price.

After luncheon Nan asked Flossie if she would like to walk over to Mrs. Power's, and talk to her about the arrangements for selling toys.

"Oh, yes," Flossie replied. "Maybe she'll show us the toys."

Mrs. Power was pleased to learn that she was to have a booth at the fair in Claremont. She asked the girls if they would like to go up to the attic and help her select the things to sell.

Nan and Flossie said this would be fun. The sisters liked old attics because they usually were full of dress-up clothes. The Bobbseys often spent rainy afternoons in their own attic and put on shows with the queer old clothes they found in the trunks.

Mrs. Power led the way to the third floor, opened a big door and switched on a light. The room was full of trunks, suitcases and boxes. The girls' eyes popped when Mrs. Power pointed out three large trunks which contained toys!

"Have you any extra special dolls with pretty faces and pretty dresses?" Flossie asked.

"Several," Mrs. Power smiled. "I'm afraid I couldn't sell them, though. But I'll show the collection to you."

She lifted the lid of one of the trunks. Nan and Flossie gasped. Lying in a row in open boxes were a group of the loveliest dolls they had ever seen. Mrs. Power picked one up.

"This isn't an ordinary doll," she said. "This was made to look exactly like the wife of the first President of our country—Martha Washington."

"She's beautiful!" Nan murmured, and Flossie asked if she could give Mrs. Washington one little tiny hug.

Then the doll was put back, and Mrs. Power pointed out the other lovely porcelain and china ladies in the trunk.

She opened another trunk. This one, she said, contained toys that might be sold.

The trunk was on top of a big box and Flossie had to stand on tiptoe to look into it. Still she could not see the contents very well, because they were halfway down. Finding a little stool, she climbed onto it and leaned over the side.

The next moment Flossie went head first down among the toys. There was a horrible sound of breaking wood!

CHAPTER XVIII

BERT'S FIGHT

NAN made a grab for her small sister, and pulled her out of the trunk. The little girl began to cry.

"I broke something!" she wailed. "I bet it was awful important, too!"

Mrs. Power leaned over and reached for the broken toy. It was a doll's cradle—a white one with a hood decorated with pink satin ribbon. One side of the cradle was splintered.

"I'm so sorry," whimpered Flossie, covering her eyes so she would not have to look at the damaged cradle.

Mrs. Power patted the little girl. She said that though the cradle was old, it was not very valuable. Besides, her son could fix it easily.

Flossie dried her eyes and smiled. Mrs. Power was so kind!

She and Nan began setting the old toys onto the floor.

"Oh, isn't this a darling little bike!" Nan exclaimed. "It has four tiny men riding on it."

The unusual toy had three wheels, a large one in front and two small ones side by side in the rear. The bicycle had a chain drive. Although there were four sets of pedals, there was only one set of handle bars.

"This toy is rather rare," Mrs. Power remarked. "It should bring a good price."

Flossie called Nan's attention to a proud-looking iron camel which was lying down. Between his two humps sat a desert rider covered from head to toe with a long robe. Mrs. Power lifted the rider off.

"The camel is really a bank," she said. "See that slot between his humps? That's where the money goes in. The toy was called a *Still Bank*."

Flossie asked if that was why the camel was lying down. Mrs. Power laughed and said she guessed that must be the reason.

Flossie lifted it from the floor and shook the toy gently. Something rattled inside.

"The camel has money inside him!" she exclaimed.

Mrs. Power turned the bank upside down and jiggled it until the coins began to slide out.

"These are very old," she said, looking at the dates on a couple of them. "I believe we'll take the money out before I sell the camel."

She gave Flossie this job, while she went on rummaging in the trunk. Soon it was empty and Mrs. Power started unpacking a second one. The first thing she took out was a quaint doll carriage, very high and narrow like a buggy.

"The umbrella on it is pretty," Flossie remarked.

Mrs. Power said this was called a parasol. A long time ago, ladies did not think it was proper to get suntanned, and did not permit the sun to shine on their babies. So, of course, little ladies did not let the sun shine on their doll babies.

"I'm going to ask my mother to buy this for me at the fair," said Flossie. "I think Marie would like to ride in it. Maybe I shouldn't let her get suntanned."

After Mrs. Power and the girls had been in the attic an hour, there were so many old toys on the floor that there was hardly room to step around.

"I had no idea I owned so many," Mrs. Power chuckled. "Nan, I'm certainly grateful to you for bringing them to my attention. If all of them can be sold, it should mean a good bit of money to the Firemen's Fair—and to me, too."

She called downstairs to her son, asking that he come up and pick out any toys which he might want to keep as family souvenirs. She selected a few herself, and then put back all that she and her son had decided to save.

"I'll have to find some way to take these toys to the fair," said Mrs. Power.

"I think Mother would be glad to take them for you," Nan said. "I'll ask her," she offered, as they started downstairs.

When they reached the first floor, Flossie happened to glance out a side window. She gasped. A man on a big gasoline mower was working in the lot where the Rootin' Tootin' Railroad was to be set up! Had the lot been sold after all?

"Somebody's using our train place!" she cried out.

Mr. Power looked out the window also. A man he had never seen before was busy cutting grass. Since Mr. Power had not hired him, he went outside at once to speak to him.

Nan and Flossie followed. When they heard that their father had sent the man to cut the grass, they laughed in relief.

"The train's coming real soon," Flossie told Mr. Power.

"Yes, I know," he replied.

As they stood watching the man on the mower, Bert Bobbsey came up with Waggo on a leash. He tied the dog to a tree, and began talking to Mr. Power about the best place to lay the track.

Presently the man cutting the grass stopped to

mop his brow and get a drink of water. Bert asked if he might run the machine around the lot.

"Did you ever operate one?" the workman asked.

"Oh, sure," Bert replied. "On my Uncle Daniel's farm."

"Then go ahead," the man smiled. "I'm going to rest awhile, anyway."

Bert guided the mower very well. Flossie watched him a few moments. Then she decided to take Waggo, who was whining, for a little walk.

Flossie had just untied him when she noticed Danny Rugg ambling up the street. As he met her, the boy made a face at Flossie.

"You thought I couldn't find out where you're going to bring your train," he taunted.

"It isn't any secret," Flossie said calmly.

Danny stood watching Bert Bobbsey run the mower. A gleam of jealousy came into Danny's eyes. He picked up a stone at the edge of the lot, and hurled it.

"Bert!" Flossie screamed, as the stone went directly toward her brother.

Bert looked up in time to duck the stone, which sailed over his head. Danny turned and dashed down the street. At the same moment Waggo jerked loose from Flossie's hand and went after him. In a couple of seconds he caught up to Danny and grabbed the seat of his pants in his sharp teeth.

"Ouch!" Danny yelled, trying to shake Waggo loose.

Bert had shut off the mower and raced down the street after Danny. He caught up and ordered Waggo to let go.

Danny doubled up his fists. "I'll get you for this!" he spluttered, and tried to hit Bert.

Bert sidestepped the blow. Then he punched Danny squarely on the chin. Danny fell down. He rose and jabbed Bert on the shoulder.

"Don't fight! Don't fight!" Flossie pleaded, racing up. She remembered many tussles between the two boys. She did not like to see them get hurt.

Bert paid no attention. He had several scores to settle with Danny. Now was a good time.

CHAPTER XIX

THE STOLEN TOY

BOYS and girls in the neighborhood began to run toward Bert and Danny to see the fight. Both lads were puffing now. Each one had struck several hard blows. Danny's nose was bleeding and Bert's lip was swollen.

Bert directed a well-aimed punch at Danny's shoulder. Down went the other boy again. He sat up, rubbing his shoulder, but did not rise.

"Had enough?" Bert asked him.

Danny hated to give up the fight, especially with other boys looking on. But he knew that Bert had the better of him this time. He staggered to his feet and leaned against a tree.

Bert did not wait for an answer. As the children cheered him, he turned and stalked back to the gasoline mower.

The man who was running the mower was busy cutting the grass again, so Bert decided to go home.

He asked Flossie if she wanted to stay awhile and play with Waggo.

The little girl, glad the fight was over, said she would. She went back to the Powers' home. As she walked in, Mrs. Power was talking to Nan about the watch which Bert had found in the old barn.

"Did Agnes Smither's picture ever help you identify the owner?" Mrs. Power asked.

Nan did not answer immediately. For a few seconds she had a faraway look in her eyes. Then she said suddenly:

"Mrs. Power, I'll bet I just solved the mystery!"

"Which one?" Flossie spoke up.

Nan replied that it had just come to her that the horrid man who had tried to take the diamond ring looked like *Agnes Smither!*

"Maybe he's her brother!" she guessed.

A sad look came over Mrs. Power's face. She said she hoped not. Agnes Smither had been a lovely woman. It would be dreadful if her brother had become a thief!

As soon as Nan and Flossie reached home, Nan told her mother her latest suspicion. Mrs. Bobbsey felt that the clue was worth following, and personally went to telephone Detective Lynch.

The policeman was very glad to receive this new information. He regretted having to report no progress on the case. The thief must be in hiding.

"Didn't you find out anything from the man who pretended to be a policeman?" Mrs. Bobbsey asked the detective.

"No. He was paid by the other man to dress up like a policeman. We're convinced he knew nothing about what the other man was really going to do. He insists he did not even know the man's name, and we believe him."

The detective did have something of importance to report. John Blaine, who had taken Danny's bicycle from the barn, had admitted being a friend of Ray Smither. He insisted, though, that he had not seen him in years.

John Blaine had gone to the housing development to look for a job, he had said, and thought someone had left the bicycle.

"We let him go," Detective Lynch said. "But I'll look him up now and check his story about Ray Smither."

Two days later the Bobbsey twins awoke in a specially happy mood. Their railroad was to be moved to the Powers' lot that day!

Sam and two other drivers were to go to the Dodge barn with Mr. Bobbsey's largest lumber truck and hoist the *Little Iron Horse,* the tender, and the passenger car aboard.

At breakfast Mr. Bobbsey suggested that his wife drive the children out to the farm ahead of time.

While they were waiting for Sam, they would enjoy seeing what had been done at the housing development.

"You won't believe it," he said.

Directly after luncheon they started off. As they neared the farm, Bert said he would open up the barn and have everything ready, so the train could be moved easily. Then suddenly he remembered that he had given the keys to his father.

"Gee," he said, provoked at himself, "we can't get into the barn until Dad comes."

"I'm sure we shan't have to wait long," said Mrs. Bobbsey. "Oh, my goodness, look over there!"

The twins could not believe so much had happened at the Dodge place during the past few days. Three small houses were standing there!

"How could they build them in such a hurry?" Freddie asked, astounded. "They grow faster than Flossie and I do!"

Mrs. Bobbsey said they were the kind of houses which are built in sections in a factory, and trucked to the places where they are to be put up.

"They have no cellars," she explained, "so it doesn't take long to get the foundations ready to set them on. And with many men working, it doesn't take but a day to put the houses together."

"They're just like great big dollhouses," said Flossie. "I think they are very cute."

Indeed, the houses were pretty. Each one was different in style and painted in such a pretty color.

The twins' mother parked the car, and they got out. As the Bobbseys stood looking at the houses, a man drove up. He asked if they were interested in buying one of the new houses.

"I guess they wouldn't be big enough for so many twins," said Flossie.

The man looked surprised. When he heard that the Bobbsey family had two sets of twins, he laughed and said he guessed the little girl was right about the houses being too small.

"Did you help build these houses?" Flossie asked him.

The man said no, but that he had come to put some decorations on them. From the back seat of his car he took out a large package and unwrapped it. Inside were several weathervanes.

"I'm going to put these on the houses," he remarked. "Maybe you would like to help me," he said to Bert.

The boy was thrilled at the possibility of climbing up and helping to set the ornaments in place. One was a donkey kicking his heels into the air. Another was a full-rigged sailing ship. Bert said he would like to adjust the sailing ship.

The man borrowed a ladder from the carpenters, and in a few minutes the donkey was stationed on top of one of the houses. He immediately turned his back on the children.

"Wind's east," the man announced. "I guess it will rain soon."

"Oh dear," said Flossie. "I don't want it to rain, because we're going to move the Rootin' Tootin' Railroad."

For the second time the man looked surprised, and had to be told what she meant. He said he hoped the barn would be opened before he had to leave. He certainly would like to get a look at the train.

"We call our engine our *Little Iron Horse* 'cause he has been living in a barn," Flossie told him. "I don't know what we'll call him when he gets moved."

The man set his ladder against the second house, and climbed up to get the place ready on the gable for the ship weathervane. Then he came down and let Bert go up to set it in place. The boy screwed it fast, and when the man inspected the work, he said Bert had done a very good job.

"Listen!" Nan said suddenly. "I hear a truck. Maybe it's Dad's!"

The children ran to look. Sure enough, Sam was driving in with the big lumber truck. The twins raced toward it to be on hand the minute the barn was unlocked.

Mr. Bobbsey drove in directly behind the truck and parked. He took the keys from his pocket, opened the side door of the old barn, and pushed open the big doors.

Bert was the first one inside. He made a beeline for the *Little Iron Horse*. A moment later the other Bobbseys heard him cry out:

"It's gone! There's nothing here!"

"What do you mean?" Nan called in alarm.

Then she saw for herself. The *Little Iron Horse*, the tender, and the passenger car of the Rootin' Tootin' Railroad were gone!

CHAPTER XX

WHERE had the little train gone? It seemed unbelievable that it was not standing in the old barn.

Bert and Nan sat down on the floor. They looked very sad. Flossie and Freddie began to cry. Finally Freddie sobbed:

"I—I just can't believe it. Our *Little Iron Horse* must be around here some place!"

"You think someone stole it?" Mrs. Bobbsey asked the twins' father.

Mr. Bobbsey looked angry. He said it was more likely that the men connected with the housing development had moved the little railroad to another spot without his permission.

"Let's ask the bulldozer man where it is, Bert," Freddie suggested.

They could see Jim McCarty working far to one side of the housing development.

"I want to go," said Flossie.

"I'll go with you," Mr. Bobbsey said. Many trucks

138

were coming and going, and the small twins might easily get in the way.

"Nan, you come, too," Flossie urged.

The children and their father trudged down a newly made street and over the plowed field until they came to where Jim McCarty was driving his bulldozer. He stopped and said:

"Hello."

Freddie blurted out that the Rootin' Tootin' Railroad was gone.

"Your railroad's gone?" the man asked in surprise.

"Somebody took it," Flossie told him. "Do you know who it was?"

Jim McCarty shook his head. "I don't know anything about it."

He suggested that they ask the foreman of the housing development.

"Where is he?" Mr. Bobbsey inquired.

Jim McCarty said the foreman was at the old Dodge home. This was now being used as an office by the development company.

The Bobbseys set off for the big white house. They found the foreman in his office. Hearing their story, the man was amazed.

"I'm terribly sorry," he said. "It makes it look bad for us. But I assure you none of my workmen moved your railroad."

Just to make doubly certain, the foreman said he

would go with the twins and their father to speak to all the workmen about the Rootin' Tootin' Railroad.

They walked around the place, inquiring if anyone had seen the train being moved or knew anything about it. No one did.

"There's just one possibility left," the foreman said. "We have a night watchman named Hogan who keeps his eye on the development. He isn't here all the time—just rides in once in a while, but he may know something about your train."

The foreman wrote Mr. Hogan's address on a slip of paper, and handed it to the twins' father. The Bobbsey family drove at once to his house.

When they reached it, the man's wife said she would see if he were awake yet. Mr. Hogan worked at night, so he had to sleep nearly all day. But it was about time for him to get up.

"Does he have his supper before he has his breakfast?" Freddie asked her.

Mrs. Hogan smiled, and said yes, her husband did everything backwards. When he got up he had his supper, and just before he went to bed he had his breakfast.

When Mr. Hogan came downstairs, he was surprised to learn that the Bobbseys thought their railroad had been stolen. The evening before, when he was going his rounds at the housing development, a large truck had driven in.

He had seen lights in the barn and heard something going on. Since he knew Mr. Bobbsey was to remove the train, he had not gone up to see who was taking it.

"I thought of course it was your lumber truck, Mr. Bobbsey," the watchman said. "You think the train has been stolen?"

"I'm sure of it," Mr. Bobbsey replied, his eyes flashing. "I know it was not your job to look after our train, but I'm mighty sorry you didn't see who was taking it away."

Mr. Hogan said he was sorry, too.

"The doors were locked," Bert spoke up. "How did the man get in?"

Mr. Hogan said he had found the wooden window open and closed it. "I guess that's how the thief got in," he said.

Bert was dismayed. He had thought the window so tightly wedged it could not be opened. And Mr. Bobbsey remarked that only a very small man could squeeze through the opening in any case.

All the Bobbseys had the same thought: how large was Ray Smither? They asked the Hogans if they knew him.

The watchman and his wife shook their heads. "I'm afraid we can't help you any," Mr. Hogan said. "Do you suspect someone named Ray Smither?"

Mr. Bobbsey said they had reason to believe he

might be the person, but he was not actually accusing him. However, if Mr. or Mrs. Hogan should ever hear of him, would they please let Mr. Bobbsey know?

The Bobbseys did not know where to look for their missing train. By this time it was probably miles and miles away from Lakeport.

When the twins' friends heard about the loss, they came over to console the twins. But this did no good. Even when Charlie rushed into the house one morning saying he knew where there was another little railroad they could ride on, they shook their heads.

"Where is it?" Bert asked without enthusiasm.

"It's going to be at the Firemen's Fair," Charlie replied. "A fireman told me."

This announcement only made the twins sadder.

"It won't be the same as our own little railroad," sighed Freddie.

"There'll never be anything in my whole life again I'll love so much as the *Little Iron Horse*," Flossie added.

Bert and Nan were quiet. They resolved that when they got to the fair, they would go nowhere near the little railroad.

Dinah did her best to cheer up the children. She baked special cakes and pies. She made cookies and puddings which they loved. But all this did no good. The children seemed to have no appetite at all.

"You simply must stop worrying about your lost railroad," Mrs. Bobbsey said a few days later. "Perhaps we'll take a little trip, and then you'll forget what happened."

The twins looked at her in amazement. How in the world could they ever forget their wonderful *Little Iron Horse?*

The twins did decide to go outdoors to play, however. As Freddie and his sisters were getting ready, Bert stepped to the back porch. He noticed a note on the floor. His name was printed on it. Opening the note quickly, he read:

"Bert Bobbsey, if you want to find out something about your missing train, answer the telephone at three o'clock this afternoon."

Bert stared at the note. Then he noticed a P. S. It said: "Don't tell your family about this, or you won't find out where the train is."

"What you doing?" Freddie asked, coming out and seeing his brother staring at the note.

Bert's first thought was that the note was a fake. Now he was not so sure. "I'll tell you later," he said, racing down the steps.

Bert had decided to see Charlie Mason and show him the note.

CHAPTER XXI

A TELLTALE CAP

IT WAS three o'clock. Bert and Charlie, alone in the Bobbsey house, sat in the living room waiting for the telephone to ring. They had decided that if Bert were told to leave the house and go anywhere, the two friends would stick together.

"Maybe nobody'll call," Charlie said three minutes later.

Then both boys jumped as the telephone bell sounded. Bert leaped to the hall to answer it.

"Hello," he said excitedly.

"Is this Bert Bobbsey?" a strange voice asked. Bert thought it sounded like a boy's voice. He had half expected it might be a man's.

"Yes," Bert replied. "Who's this?"

The stranger did not answer. Bert motioned for Charlie to come to the telephone. Charlie tiptoed forward, and Bert held the receiver so both of them could listen.

The strange speaker went on, "Come to Beaver Hollow to find out about your train."

Bert asked what time he should be there, and if it would be all right for him to bring somebody along.

"I told you not to say anything to anybody!"

"I didn't say anything to my family," said Bert. "How about it?"

Again there was silence on the other end of the line, as if the speaker were consulting a pal about what to do. At last he said Bert could bring one boy with him, but if he told the police or any other grownups, he would be sorry.

"Be there at five o'clock."

The speaker hung up, and Bert and Charlie sat down to discuss the affair. Charlie was convinced that this was no joke. He was afraid Bert Bobbsey might get himself in trouble if he went to Beaver Hollow.

"How would they know if you did tell someone else?" he asked.

"You're right," Bert agreed. "I'll leave a note for Mother. If anything *should* happen, she can send help to us. But I don't think it will."

Beaver Hollow was in a well-known woods where the children of Lakeport often went on hikes and picnics. There surely would be other people in the woods, so it would be perfectly safe for Bert and Charlie to go alone.

At four o'clock the two boys set off confidently, without any thought of danger. It was a rather long walk to the woods, so they decided to take a bus. Getting off several minutes later at a little-used path, they set out among the trees. Bert knew a shortcut from this point to a trail which led toward Beaver Hollow.

One thing which he and Charlie had not remembered was that after five o'clock people were not supposed to be in these woods and particularly around Beaver Hollow. But by not sticking to the main trail, the boys were not seen by the watchman at the entrance.

"I don't see why anybody would bring you way out here to tell you about your railroad," Charlie said presently.

"I don't either," Bert agreed. "That's why I think this whole thing is a joke. And what's more, I'm sure it's Danny Rugg and some other boy who are playing the joke. It's up to us to get ahead of them."

"How?" Charlie asked.

Bert did not know exactly, but he suggested that he and Charlie watch carefully as they went along and not walk into any trap. Danny, if he were the one playing the trick, certainly would have set some kind of trap.

The boys walked on and on. Nothing happened.

They saw no one, and heard nothing but the usual sounds of the woods in late afternoon.

"Say," said Charlie suddenly, "maybe Danny just wanted to get rid of you while he plays some kind of a joke on Flossie or Freddie."

"Or Nan," Bert added.

For a moment he was ready to turn back. Then he realized that he was too far from home to keep Danny from carrying out such a trick.

"Let's go on to Beaver Hollow," Charlie urged. "Maybe someone will be there after all to tell you about the train."

"Okay."

It was a long hike. When they were about a quarter of a mile from the stream which ran through Beaver Hollow, the two boys sat down to rest. Bert's eyes suddenly spied something on the ground. He got up, walked over, and picked it up.

"What is it?" Charlie asked.

"A boy's cap. A new one, too. I don't think it's been here long."

There was nothing about the red and white cap to identify the owner. They wondered if he was hiding among the trees and spying on them.

Bert and Charlie looked around. They could see no one, but they had a strange feeling that they were being watched.

"I don't like this," Bert spoke up. "Let's separate. You circle to the left and I'll go to the right. If somebody's hiding, maybe we can find him."

The two boys scouted around for several minutes, still finding no one. They walked on, and in a short time came to Beaver Hollow. A small stream ran through it. They searched this place also. No one put in an appearance. By now it was quite late and both boys were getting tired of waiting for something to happen. Bert felt sure Danny Rugg was behind the scheme.

"Well, what say we go back home?" Charlie suggested. "I certainly don't want to tell any of the fellows I came out here just because a note told me to. Let's keep it to ourselves."

"I'll agree with you about keeping it a secret," Bert replied. "But let's not go yet. We ought to get something out of this trip," he grinned. "Let's try to catch some fish."

"Okay," Charlie said, pulling out his pocketknife to cut a pole.

The two boys cut branches from a small tree and stripped them down. Using string and some wire Bert had in his pocket, they attached them to the poles. Then the boys started digging for worms.

Charlie was the first to find one, and fastened it to the wire. He cast his line and stood waiting for a nibble.

In a moment Bert, too, had baited his line, and stood beside Charlie, hoping for a bite. Presently he felt a tug.

The boy played his line as best he could, leaning far over the water. Slowly he pulled it in.

"I've got him!" he cried gleefully.

The next second a thrashing speckled trout lay on the bank.

"Gee, I hope I get one," said Charlie.

The words were scarcely out of his mouth when he, too, felt a tug. He had just laid his trout on the bank when the two boys were startled by a sound across the little stream.

"Help! Help!" a faraway voice seemed to be crying.

The two boys listened intently. There was no mistaking the second time they heard the cry.

"Who are you?" Bert shouted.

For a moment there was no reply, then he was startled to hear: "Freddie! Come and help me quick!"

Bert did not wait even to kick off his shoes. Freddie must have found out from his mother where the boys had gone and tried to find them. Now he was in trouble. Bert dashed across the shallow stream, with Charlie right after him.

"Where are you, Freddie?" Bert called excitedly.

A faint voice answered, "Keep coming straight!"

The boys made a wild dash through the thick underbrush. They had not gone far when the two of them fell flat on their faces. Something they had not seen had tripped them.

Bert scrambled up and started on. He was surprised that Charlie did not rise at once. Running back, he found that Charlie had hit his head on a stone and was unconscious.

CHAPTER XXII

A MYSTERY SOLVED

AS BERT wondered whom to help first—Freddie or Charlie—he heard someone giggle in the bushes ahead.

"This *is* a trick," Bert thought, "and a mean one, too!"

Sure now that Freddie was not in the woods, he ran to the stream, took out a handkerchief and wet it thoroughly. Dashing back, he laid it on Charlie's forehead. Then he began to rub the boy's wrists.

In a few moments Charlie opened his eyes. He looked around dazed.

"What happened?" he asked.

Bert told him. He suggested that Charlie lie still, while he made a search for the person who had giggled.

"Charlie, look at this!" he exclaimed presently, picking up a mass of trailing vines.

Several vines had been woven together to make a rather long rope. There was no doubt now in Bert

Bobbsey's mind what had taken place. Someone had made the rope and strung it between two trees, then called the boys so they would deliberately trip over it.

As Charlie waited, Bert dashed among the trees and bushes, trying to find out who it might have been.

"I'll bet it was Danny," he told himself.

But whether it was Danny or someone else, the person proved to be clever enough not to be spotted. At last Bert gave up the search. He returned to Charlie, who insisted he felt able to walk now.

They recrossed the stream, picked up their fish, and started for home. Finally they came to the main road and boarded a bus. Bert went to Charlie's house with him to be sure he was all right.

When Bert arrived at his own home, it was just past suppertime. His worried parents asked what had happened. When Bert reached the part in the story about Freddie, his small brother opened his eyes wide.

"I wasn't in the woods," he insisted.

"It sounded like you, though," said Bert, "so I had to go look for you."

Nan was thoughtful. She could not figure out why anyone would play such a dangerous trick.

"Bert, did you keep the cap you found?" she asked.

He pulled it from his pocket.

"Good," said Nan. "Why don't you wear it a few days? Maybe the boy who lost the cap will claim it and give himself away."

"That's a good idea," Bert said. "I'll wear it to the Firemen's Fair tomorrow."

The fair was to open at two o'clock next day, but the people who were to have exhibits had planned to arrive in the morning to get them ready.

"What time are we going to Mrs. Power's for the toys?" Flossie asked her mother.

"I believe we should be there by nine o'clock," Mrs. Bobbsey replied. "It will take a long time to arrange everything on the shelves."

She was surprised that Freddie did not tease to go along. It was Dinah who found out why not. Freddie told her that he was afraid he might have to pass the little train which was to be at the fair. It would make him too sad about their stolen railroad. He would not go to the fair until there were lots of people around.

"Then they'll be in the way and I won't see the train," he said, and Dinah smiled.

The other children felt just as bad as Freddie did. They did not even talk about the Rootin' Tootin' Railroad any more.

But the next morning Bert did go down to the police station and ask Detective Lynch if any clues had turned up. The policeman said he had just received some information which he was going to track down this very day.

When Bert returned, he found that his mother, Nan, and Flossie had already left for Mrs. Power's home. The toys she was willing to sell were wrapped and put in boxes. It did not take the group long to pack them in Mrs. Bobbsey's car and drive off to Claremont.

There was hustle and bustle at the Firemen's Fair. Trucks were being driven in with all sorts of articles piled on them. People were running here and there with ladders and tools. Booths were being decorated with fancy streamers and bunting.

"It's 'citing, isn't it?" Flossie remarked, as they showed their pass to the man at the gate and went in.

"Yes, it is," her mother replied. "I had no idea the fair would be so large."

They drove to the booth which had been assigned to Mrs. Power, and unloaded the boxes. Flossie was fascinated as each toy was brought out. There were many which she had not seen before.

"Oh, look at that darling little kitchen," she said, examining an old-fashioned tin kitchen, with a wood-burning stove, and red pots and pans hanging on the wall.

"Here is something quite lovely," said Mrs. Power, as she unwrapped a rather large package.

"You may think that walking dolls are something new, but this one was made way back in 1862. It has a long, long name."

"What is it?" Flossie asked.

Mrs. Power laughed, and said, "Autoperipatekos."

"Oh my goodness!" said Mrs. Bobbsey. "You don't mean that's the name of the doll?"

Mrs. Power explained that this was only the trade name. This beautiful doll's name was Sally. "I think what that long word really means is that this doll can walk. Here, I'll show you."

She wound it up and set it on the counter of the booth. With a jerky motion, Sally paraded across the counter.

"Oh, she's scrumptious!" Flossie cried out. Turning to her mother, she said, "Can't we . . . ?"

Mrs. Bobbsey's eyes twinkled. " . . . can't we buy Sally?" she finished the sentence. "I thought you wanted the doll carriage."

"Sally made me change my mind," Flossie giggled.

Mrs. Bobbsey picked up the price tag which Mrs. Power had put on Sally, and said it cost a good deal of money. She would have to ask Flossie's father what he thought about it.

As the other toys were set in place, some on shelves at the back of the booth and others on the counter, many people came to look at the exhibit.

Several women declared that it was by far the most attractive booth in the whole Firemen's Fair.

"Goody, goody!" Flossie exclaimed. "Everybody'll make lots of money!"

"I hope so," said Mrs. Power. Now that she was in the spirit of the thing, she wanted the sale to be a great success.

She had brought her lunch, and said she would stay right there to guard the exhibit, while Mrs. Bobbsey took the girls home.

At one-thirty the whole Bobbsey family started back to the fair. Flossie kept tight hold of her father's hand and when they reached Claremont, led him straight to Mrs. Power's booth.

"Well!" he exclaimed, seeing the exhibit. "This is even better than I thought it would be."

"It sure is swell!" Bert burst out.

He had not thought he would be very interested in the toys, but now as he looked at old fire engines, locomotives, and a target board which changed pictures whenever one of the pictures was hit, he was intrigued by them.

"Here's Sally," Flossie pointed out to her father. "Please, can't we buy her?"

Mr. Bobbsey said he did not want to spend so much for one toy.

"You forget, Little Fat Fairy," he added, "that there are four of you children. If I should pay this much for a toy for each one of you, I'm afraid my pockets would be empty."

Nan stepped forward. She told her father that she admired the doll almost as much as Flossie did and would like it for the girls' bedroom. She would be glad to put her share toward Sally, and the sisters could enjoy her together.

"All right then," Mr. Bobbsey finally conceded. "I'll buy Sally for you girls."

Flossie clapped her hands in glee. As Mrs. Power handed the doll to her, she said that the Little Fat Fairy had been her first customer.

Freddie selected an old fire engine which would pump water. Bert decided that he would like the target that changed pictures.

As the children walked around the fair grounds with their parents, the twins took great pains to avoid the spot where they could hear the little railroad running. Bert went off by himself to see if any of his friends were at the fair. As he passed a shooting gallery, he stopped to watch a man knock down moving clay pigeons. Alongside the man stood Danny Rugg.

Bert began to whistle. Danny turned around. Then, without thinking, he dashed toward Bert Bobbsey and cried out:

"What are you doing with my cap?"

CHAPTER XXIII

AN AMAZING DISCOVERY

DANNY had given himself away! Bert Bobbsey had hard work to keep from laughing.

"So you dropped your cap in the woods, eh, Danny?" he asked. "And who helped you rig up that vine rope? Jim Walker?" Jim was one of Danny's friends who was almost as full of tricks as Danny himself.

The other boy winced and Bert knew he had guessed the truth. Danny realized he had given himself away. He turned, and pretended not to hear what Bert had said to him. Bert grabbed him by the shoulder.

"Look, Danny, you think you're smart, don't you? But you're not. And listen; if you know anything about where our railroad went, you'd better tell me!"

"Why should I tell you?" Danny retorted.

By this time several older people had gathered

around the boys. Danny began to feel uncomfort-
able.

"I'd better scram," Danny thought, and dashed
back of one of the booths.

Bert ran after him, and caught Danny by his coat.

"Tell me what I want to know," Bert shouted angrily.

"I'll tell you one thing," Danny said, trying to
get away from Bert's grip. "You'd better stay away
from the little train at this fair, or you'll be sorry!"

"Why?" Bert asked him.

" 'Cause the man there doesn't like you."

Bert was so surprised to hear this that he re-
laxed his hold. Danny yanked loose and ran off.
He disappeared in the crowd.

"Why'd Danny run away?" Freddie asked, coming up with the rest of his family.

His brother told them what Danny had said about
the man who was running the train.

"What do you think he meant?" Bert asked.

Nan guessed that Danny was just trying to be
smart. Her parents agreed, and suggested that the
children forget about Danny and have some fun.
Mr. and Mrs. Bobbsey took the small twins off for
rides on the ponies.

As the older twins walked along looking at the exhibits, they came to a booth where two boys, dressed

as clowns, were doing a juggling act with balls. As one of them turned around, Bert exclaimed:

"Jackie Braun!"

He went up to the counter and spoke to Jackie, who was glad to see Bert and Nan again. Nan asked where his father was.

"Running the train," Jackie answered.

He said he and his father had had hard luck recently. They had not been able to take in enough money on their juggling act to make it pay. Mr. Braun had decided he must find some other work to add to their income.

"So he's running the train," Jackie concluded. Then he introduced the other boy to Bert and Nan. "This is my cousin, Bud Braun," he said.

"Hello," said Bud. "You live around here?"

"No. Lakeport," Bert replied.

Jackie said he must get back to work. In a loud voice he called out:

"Right this way, everybody! Step this way! Prizes for everyone!"

As people came forward, the boy announced that the prizes were hanging in the back of the booth. They would go to the people who could juggle with him and not drop the balls.

Several boys stepped behind the counter and tried the little act. But they dropped the balls each time, though they had three chances.

Nan nudged Bert's arm. "Why don't you try it, Bert?" she asked. "You learned lots of tricks from old Sing Foo out at the Mystery Mansion."

Bert had not done any juggling recently, but he thought perhaps it would be fun to try anyway. He went behind the counter and took a turn. At first the balls would not stay in his hand, but by the time Bert got to his third chance, he was juggling almost as well as Jackie. Jackie gave Bert a little compass as his prize.

"Where in the world did you learn how to juggle so well?" Bud asked him. "You'd better take my place. I'm not very good at juggling yet."

Bert said he would like to, but he could not travel around the country the way Jackie did. He had to stay in Lakeport and go to school.

"Say, Jackie, what do you do about school?" Bert asked.

Jackie looked down at the counter. A sad look came over his face. When he did not speak, Bud answered for him:

"Jackie's mother used to be his teacher. She died a few months ago."

"Oh, that's too bad," said Bert and Nan together.

Jackie told them that his mother had been a very fine teacher, so that he had really been ahead of his grade in school. Once in a while, when they stayed in a town for several weeks, he would go to the public school there. He had never had any trouble keeping up with the classes.

"But I don't know what I'm going to do now," he said, tears coming into his eyes. "My father said he would try to teach me, but he's always so busy, he doesn't have time."

Bud Braun said his cousin could live with him and go to school but Jackie would not leave his father. There was no more chance to talk about Jackie's schooling, because people were gathering to see the show.

Jackie juggled the balls several times and then started to throw them to his cousin one by one. Bud managed to catch the first two, but dropped the third and fourth. He became so confused as Jackie kept throwing the balls at him, that he dropped them all! The crowd roared with laughter.

"The World's Clumsiest Clown!" Jack called gaily, trying to cover up for Bud. But he knew his cousin would not be able to continue with the act and wondered what to do.

The people continued to laugh as Bud kept fumbling with the balls. Jackie bent over and whispered to Bert:

"Do you think you could help me out? There's an extra clown suit in back of the booth."

"I'll try," said Bert. He felt very happy to think that Jackie should invite him to help in his act.

He quickly told Nan what he was going to do, then disappeared behind the booth and put on the clown suit. He bobbed through the curtain, and took over the little act.

Bert just did the straight throwing and juggling, but Jackie imitated what his father used to do. He let the ball land on his head, on his back, and on each shoulder. It was amazing how he could bounce them back to Bert.

"Those boys are sure good!" said a man who was standing in the crowd. "I wish I could do that. Who are they anyway?"

Nan wondered if she should tell the man that one of them was her brother. She was very proud of what Bert was doing. How fortunate it was that the old Chinese had shown him some tricks!

Before Nan had a chance to say anything, she felt someone pushing against her. Looking down, she saw Freddie and Flossie, who had wormed their way through the crowd.

"Wow!" Freddie cried. "That's my brother throwing the balls!"

Mr. and Mrs. Bobbsey stood in the background. They, too, were amazed at their son's accomplishment. They had seen him do a little juggling act Sing Foo had shown him, and a few other tricks, but they had not realized he was as good as this.

Nan told her parents what Jackie had said about

losing his mother, and how he had no one to teach him now. She also told them that his father was running the miniature railroad.

"Maybe we ought to go and take a ride on it to help him out," she said. "When Bert gets through, let's ask him."

In a few minutes Bud Braun changed places with Bert. Then Mr. Bobbsey bought tickets for all his family to go in side the enclosure where the little train was running around a circular track. The whistle gave two long blasts, one short, then one more long blast.

"The train's coming to a public crossing," thought Bert, recognizing the signal.

The Bobbseys had to wait for the train to complete its run before they heard the one long blast which meant the engine was approaching the station. As it puffed up the track toward them, Freddie's eyes suddenly grew very large.

"Daddy!" he shouted excitedly. "That's our own Rootin' Tootin' Railroad."

The Bobbseys stared. There was no question about it. Coming toward them was their *Little Iron Horse!*

CHAPTER XXIV

AN EXCITING PLAN

BOYS and girls waiting for rides on the little railroad crowded around Freddie Bobbsey as he made his exclamation.

"That's our stolen train!" he screamed.

"Shh!" Mrs. Bobbsey said to her small son. "We may be making a big mistake. Let's get closer and look at the little railroad before we say anything more."

Freddie's shouting had been heard by Mr. Braun. He jumped down from the tender and came over directly to the Bobbseys. He recognized the twins at once, and asked what the trouble was.

It was hard for them to keep still, especially Freddie. But they remained silent while Mr. Bobbsey told Mr. Braun that they had owned a miniature railroad exactly like this one, and that it had disappeared.

"I suppose you've had this railroad a long time?" Mr. Bobbsey remarked.

165

"No, I haven't," Mr. Braun replied. "As a matter of fact, two other men and I bought this railroad only recently."

"Around here?" Mr. Bobbsey questioned.

Mr. Braun said he had not seen the little train until it had been delivered to him at the fair grounds.

Freddie could not keep still any longer. "It's our train, I know it's our train!" he burst out. "Bert, look at that scratch on the smokestack. Our Rootin' Tootin' Railroad had a scratch on the smokestack!"

A still larger crowd had gathered around the little group, and Mr. Braun was very much embarrassed. He assured the Bobbseys that he had bought the train in good faith.

"I had no idea I might be buying stolen property," he said, a worried frown coming over his forehead.

He said a man named Smith had come to him with the suggestion that Mr. Braun join a traveling entertainment group. The group wanted to add a miniature railroad to their show, and if Mr. Braun would buy one which was in storage, he would be able to join the show.

"So I borrowed some money from a couple of friends of mine, and bought the train," Mr. Braun explained. "I thought of course Mr. Smith was honest. Now I don't know what to do."

He said he did not have enough money to pay

back his friends, if the train really belonged to the Bobbseys.

Freddie tugged at his mother's hand and whispered, "Why don't we get a policeman?"

Mr. Braun, hearing him, begged that they wait a little while until he could figure out what to do.

Nan took her father aside. "Dad," she said, "until we find Mr. Smith, why don't we let Mr. Braun run the train and make money? The Firemen's Fair is going to get some of it anyway."

"You're very thoughtful," said Mr. Bobbsey. "Mr. Braun seems to be honest. I'll take your advice."

He told Jackie's father that while the Firemen's Fair was in progress, he should run the train and make all the money he could. In the meantime, they would try to straighten out the matter.

Mr. Braun was very grateful for the new arrangement. He said he would leave everything to Mr. Bobbsey, but he hoped that Jackie would not have to suffer for his father's innocent mistake.

"He won't suffer," Mr. Bobbsey said, "but if Mr. Smith should turn up here, be sure to see that he is held until you notify me. What does he look like?"

"Middle age. Kind of heavy set. His hair—well, it was—"

Bert and Nan had not been paying attention. They had been holding a whispered conversation on the side. Now they were ready to put a plan into action. Nan was to telephone Detective Lynch to bring the watch with the picture in it and show it to Mr. Braun.

"And I'll go find Danny Rugg," said Bert. "You remember, he told me not to come near the train. I'll bet anything he knows more about this than we think he does."

The two children dashed off. When Nan telephoned Lakeport Police Headquarters, she was told that Detective Lynch was in Claremont and had the watch with him. He had picked up a good lead that Ray Smither was in that town.

"We'll get in touch with Lynch at once and send him to the Firemen's Fair," the police captain told her.

"I'll meet him at the gate," Nan said.

It was not long before the surprised detective arrived, and hurried with Nan toward the Rootin' Tootin' Railroad.

"I said you Bobbsey twins would solve this mystery before I did," the detective smiled.

Nan's parents were amazed to see him and to hear that it was their own daughter who had brought him there with such speed.

"I was just going to phone you a full description of Mr. Smith and how he sold our train to Mr. Braun," Mr. Bobbsey said to the detective.

The small twins were having a ride behind the

Little Iron Horse. **Mr.** Bobbsey waited until the ride was over, then called to Mr. Braun. He stopped the train and came over.

"Did Mr. Smith look anything like the woman in this picture?" Detective Lynch asked him, as he opened the back of the old watch.

Mr. Braun looked at the photograph several seconds. Then he said that Mr. Smith did look very much like the woman in the picture. Who was she?

"We understand her name was Agnes Smither," Mr. Bobbsey replied. "She's not living now. We think that the man you know as Mr. Smith may be her brother. His right name is Ray Smither."

Just then Bert came dashing up. Alongside him was Danny Rugg, and just behind them was a policeman. Danny looked very frightened.

"Dad!" said Bert. "Danny's going to tell us where we can find the man who stole our train!"

CHAPTER XXV

A THIEF AND A CLOWN

WHAT a lot of excitement there was! Seeing the policeman, people crowded around to find out what had happened.

"I think we'd better go into one of the small tents over there, and talk this over quietly," the policeman suggested.

He led the way to a tent where the committee for the Firemen's Fair had been holding its meetings. Then he told Danny to tell his story to the others.

"I—I didn't think I was doing anything wrong," Danny whimpered. "The man asked me to climb through the window in the barn, because he was too big."

As Danny paused, Detective Lynch asked him if he did not know what the man was going to do in the barn. Danny shook his head.

"If I'd known he was going to steal the train, I wouldn't have told him where the window was."

"You told him where the window was?" Bert Bobbsey spoke up.

Danny had not meant to give away this information, but it was too late to deny it now. He said he had found out about the wooden window from Freddie. At five o'clock one afternoon Danny had gone out to the barn to look over the housing development, and perhaps get inside the barn and play with the train.

"While I was there, a man came up and asked me who I was," the boy went on. "After I told him, he said didn't I know the Bobbseys? I said yes, I knew Bert and the others.

"After a while he asked me if I knew any way to get into the barn. Maybe I knew where a key was hidden. I told him I didn't, but I knew where there was a secret window."

Danny admitted that the man had given him some money to climb in the window after he had hammered it open. Then he had asked Danny to unlock the big front doors.

"He said he worked for the housing development," Danny revealed. "I didn't know he was going to take the train."

"How do you know he's the one who took the

train?" Detective Lynch asked him. "Did you see him take it?"

Danny said no. In fact, the man had not gone into the barn while Danny was there. When the boy came out of the building, he saw him talking to another man in a truck which later drove off. He had not seen the other man's face. Then Danny had gone back to Lakeport.

"I don't know anything else," Danny concluded. "I want to go home."

"Just a minute, son," Detective Lynch spoke up. "I think you may know a few more things that you haven't told us."

Danny insisted he knew nothing more, but Detective Lynch finally got more of the story from him. The most important thing he found out was that Danny had heard the man call, as the truck was leaving:

"I'll meet you at Tabor's."

Tabor's! Could this be the old Tabor farm about halfway between Claremont and Lakeport, Detective Lynch wondered. The Tabor family was away, he knew.

Suddenly he stood up, saying he wanted to make a telephone call. Everyone was to stay right there until he came back.

While he was gone, Bert asked Danny a few more

questions. Danny confessed that he had written the note asking Bert to come into the woods, so he could tell him his suspicion that the man might have stolen the train. But he had become afraid and changed his mind.

Jim had been with Danny, and the two boys had decided to have some fun and trip Bert and Charlie with the vine.

"It's too bad, Danny, that you didn't tell your story when you were first suspicious," Mr. Bobbsey spoke up sternly.

In half an hour Detective Lynch returned. To the Bobbseys' surprise he led in two men, handcuffed together. He said the short, stout one with a scar on his right hand was Ray Smither—the man who had taken the diamond ring from Nan! The other one the children recognized as John Blaine, the stranger who had taken Danny's bicycle.

"These men were out at the Tabor place all right," he announced. "I telephoned to have them arrested. Both of them have confessed that they stole the train. Unfortunately, they've spent a good deal of the money they got for it. But I'll let them tell their own story."

Ray Smither said that he was very much ashamed of what he had done. He had had hard luck recently, and had taken to stealing.

"I used to work for a carnival company," he said. "That's how I knew they wanted to add a little railroad to their acts. When I heard about the Bobbsey twins' train, through my friend John Blaine, I could not resist taking it."

Ray Smither said it had been easy to steal most of the track some time before he took the train, because the lock on the side door of the barn was not difficult to open. Later, after the padlock was put on, he could not get in.

Smither had found out about the window some time earlier. He had only pretended to Danny that he did not know where it was. He never should have asked the boy to help him get into the barn, he realized now.

"John Blaine and I used the Tabors' truck that night and carted the train away," he explained.

"Do you know who dumped hay down on my friend and me?" Bert asked.

"I did," John Blaine confessed. "I climbed in the window. Ray had sold me his old watch and I dropped it there."

"What about the diamond ring you tried to take?" Nan asked Ray Smither.

The two prisoners said they did not know who owned it. Smither had been peeking through a crack in the window at the time Nan found it. The diamond ring would belong to her if no one claimed it within a certain time.

As the policeman led his prisoners away, Detective Lynch stopped to speak to the Bobbseys. He said it would be up to them to decide what to do about Mr. Braun and their little railroad. Mr. Bobbsey concluded that he and his family had better go home and talk the matter over.

"I'd like to help Jackie," Bert spoke up after they were home and the little conference had started. "Maybe we could let the Brauns use the train part of the time, Dad."

"Sure," said Freddie.

His father nodded. He said that since it was very snowy in Lakeport during the winter, it would be only during the summer months that the little railroad could be outdoors and running.

"How would it be if we lend Mr. Braun your railroad during the winter?" he asked. "He could join the carnival and use the train while they're traveling in the South. Then he could bring it back to Lakeport for the summer."

Flossie clapped her hands. "Then we could see Jackie do his tricks," she said.

"Nan, what are you thinking about?" her mother asked. "You haven't said a word."

Her daughter laughed. "I was thinking," she

said, "how nice it would be if Jackie could have Mr. Power as a tutor."

"That's a very fine idea, Nan," Mrs. Bobbsey agreed, smiling.

Nan went on eagerly, "Mr. Power could run the Rootin' Tootin' Railroad for Mr. Braun. And then Jackie and his father could do their juggling act together again."

"And Mr. Power could fix the *Little Iron Horse* every time he broke down," Freddie called out excitedly.

That evening, at the Bobbseys' invitation, the Powers came over. How surprised they were to hear Nan's suggestion!

"Why, I'd like to teach Jackie very much," said the lame young man. "And run the little train, too."

The following afternoon he and his mother went to the Firemen's Fair with the Bobbseys. Mrs. Power had sold all her toys, so she had closed her booth.

When they reached the little railroad, Mr. Braun stopped the engine and stepped down. He knew from the smiling faces of the Bobbseys that they had pleasant news for him.

"We have an awful important secret to tell you," said Flossie eagerly.

The twins' father asked Nan to tell the "secret."

Mr. Braun was very grateful to be able to use the

little train for part of the year. And he was interested in the plan for a tutor for Jackie.

The boy and his father met Mrs. Power and her son, and after some discussion Clinton Power agreed to travel with them and teach Jackie. The biggest surprise came when Clinton announced that Mrs. Power would go along too.

"I've always wanted to travel," said Mrs. Power delightedly.

"And I think Jackie needs some mothering," the boy's father smiled.

What a happy day for the Bobbsey twins! Before leaving for home, they took ride after ride behind the *Little Iron Horse*. It seemed as if they could not get enough rides!

Jackie Braun was excited, too. Everything was coming out all right for his father and himself. He hopped aboard the Rootin' Tootin' Railroad and called to Bert:

"Hey! Catch these!"

Jackie pulled the juggling balls from his pocket and pitched them to Bert. How the people standing along the track laughed!

The two boys put on a perfect juggling act and did not drop one of the balls, even though Mr. Braun ran the *Little Iron Horse* round and round the track as fast as he dared go.

"I never had so much fun," Flossie giggled.

"I never did either," said Freddie. His father had bought him a light cane at the fair. Freddie set it on the end of his finger and twirled it madly.

"Look!" he cried. "I'm a clown, too, for the Rootin' Tootin' Railroad!"

When Bert Bobbsey's power boat model wins the Lakeport competition, he takes his boat to the big race at Whitesail Harbor. The whole Bobbsey family goes along, and the fun and exciting adventures they have there make a story you won't want to miss—

THE BOBBSEY TWINS
AT WHITESAIL HARBOR

$4 \div 2 + 16 =$

$78 \times 5 \div 3 =$

$3 \quad \div 12 =$

$\div 7 =$

$\div 7 =$